THE MYSTERY OF
Beautiful Nell Cropsey

THE MYSTERY OF

Beautiful Nell Cropsey

A NONFICTION NOVEL

Bland Simpson

The University of North Carolina Press

Chapel Hill & London

Manufactured in the

United States of America

Library of Congress

Cataloging-in-Publication Data

Simpson, Bland.

The mystery of beautiful Nell Cropsey :

a nonfiction novel / by Bland Simpson.

p.   cm.

ISBN 0-8078-2120-9 (alk. paper).—

ISBN 0-8078-4432-2 (pbk. : alk. paper)

1. Cropsey, Nell, d. 1901.   2. Murder victims—

North Carolina—Elizabeth City—Biography.

3. Wilcox, Jim.   4. Murderers—North Carolina—

Elizabeth City—Biography.   5. Murder—

North Carolina—Elizabeth City.   I. Title.

HV6534.E45C767   1993

364.1'523'09756142—dc20   93-3324

CIP

The paper in this book meets the guidelines

for permanence and durability of the Committee

on Production Guidelines for Book Longevity of

the Council on Library Resources.

97   96   95   94   93   5   4   3   2   1

For Ann Cary Simpson

who came from Carteret County

land of white boats

and brought me home

‹

CONTENTS

ILLUSTRATIONS

1901

And the angel said unto me, Wherefore didst thou marvel? I will tell thee the mystery of the woman, and of the beast that carrieth her, which hath the seven heads and ten horns.—Revelation 17:7

There is a rope some two or three generations in length, knotted near but not exactly in the middle, with an unraveling off in either direction. The knot in the unraveled rope is the moment central to a celebrated mystery, a national sensation in its day. This is the tale of that moment and the strands of time that pulled taut just then and, knotting, separated it from all the rest. By now, the mystery of Beautiful Nell Cropsey is almost a folktale, a ballad of lovers, as newspaper clippings yellow and ten thousand conversations echo across the century.

THE SEARCH

TALK

Word traveled fast in a river town with thirteen saloons. It spread with alacrity and gaining excitement through the oyster-shucking and canning houses
of Elizabeth City, North Carolina. They were well into
the *r* months there in November, and the 1901 oystering
season was on. The hundreds of workers who spent their
days with the slime and smell of a hundred-fifty-thou-
sand gallons of oysters a season needed something to
talk about there in the long frame shuckhouses built on
the Pasquotank River's horseshoe bend.

They talked about Nell Cropsey and Jim Wilcox.

Word spread into the textile mills, down the lines of
spinning bobbins whose mistresses were at the very mo-

ment of this frightful entertainment fighting and winning a price war against the northern mills over spun goods, and that victory was being bought with their deft fingers and keen eyesight and browned lungs. There was gossip on those battle lines about a girl, Nell Cropsey, who had been sweetheart to Jim Wilcox since the Cropseys came down from Brooklyn, New York, three-and-a-half years ago.

—Wasn't it his daddy used to be county sheriff? What on earth do you reckon happened?

—What about that mysterious burglar last month and the month before? It could have been him got the girl and not Wilcox after all, what do you think? You know the one. The degenerate burglar who touched women when they were asleep and always ran at the first alarm so they never got a description of him. Could have been him got Nell Cropsey and not Jim Wilcox, what do you say?

—He was the last to see her, though, far as we know.

Word spread through the sawmills and planing mills along the rivershore from Charles Creek to Knobbs Creek. The men talked, the men who kept the pressure on the boilers that drove the pistons and turned the belts and drove the bigtooth blades against the logs. Everywhere it was piney-smelling, and the men in the mills turning out hundreds of thousands of board feet a year talked about the pretty girl Nell Cropsey and the man Jim Wilcox who wasn't saying much.

—Weren't it one of his kin killed that Brothers fellow down at Newbegun a few years back?

—Could be she got in a little trouble and he had to send her away. Or she just run away on her own.

—Maybe she drowned herself if she was in that kind of trouble. He was the last to see her and he says she was crying—maybe she drowned herself in the river.

Word spread into the cypress and gum swamps through work of the getters, the hundreds of men who spent most all their time out in the woods and swamps securing timber for the insatiable mill blades. Into the remote reaches of that two-thousand-square-mile jungle, the Great Dismal Swamp, the mire that separated Elizabeth City from Norfolk, Virginia.

—Before the War, the slave that cut and ran hid out there, didn't he? The convict that busted his chain, law wouldn't go in after him, would they? Reckon Nell Cropsey could have got up in there somewhere to hide out?

—That boy Wilcox sent her up there maybe, or took her gainst her will. You hear they arrested him for kidnap? And it was his daddy that was the sheriff.

—Yep, that's him, and it was his uncle killed a man. Keep your eyes open for her—don't guess a swamp rat like you'd mind seeing a pretty young gal back up this way, hunh?

—Not at all. Say, how bout bringin me some coffee next time you get up this way?

—Sure will, sure will.

Word spread like that back into the swamps where the slaves had run, where convicts had run—mightn't Nell Cropsey run there too? Back deep toward the lake at the heart of the great Swamp, where the ghost of an Indian girl searched each night for her lost lover, by firefly lamp, gliding in her white canoe.

And word spread far beyond those low tidelands, as the dailies in the big eastern cities of Baltimore and Philadelphia and New York played up the mystery till Nell Cropsey and Jim Wilcox were the talk of the nation and the booming little river port of Elizabeth City was suddenly on the map.

Lord, the fulminations that were to rain down upon Jim Wilcox. For time closed around that moment like a circle round the sun, or stood like the moon before it, and how could anyone know the fashion in which the circle had closed, or whether the moment of Nell's disappearance had brought him within or cast him without? And if without, how were any to know, to the satisfaction that brings belief, that Wilcox was outside like the rest trying to peer in?

All his life he claimed he had left her crying on her front porch, and all his life he was doubted.

—Why didn't you see her back to the door and see her safe inside? they asked.

—If I'd a known all this trouble was going to come of it, Jim Wilcox answered, I would have.

The sick old sandy-haired man Jim Wilcox, lying on a dirty bunk with a shotgun by his side, looked back across thirty-three years, half of them in prison, and formed the whisper words: I would have.

Jim Wilcox

Lying here makes me think of it.

Thirty-three years ago if it was a day.

Mama was shaking me, the way she always had to when she wanted me to get up. They put it up against me in the papers that I was a light sleeper and even a carriage going by down on Shepard Street could of woke me. That I was a light sleeper pretending to be in a deep slumber when they come, pretending on account of I was scared bout what I'd done—or what they *said* I'd done.

They said I carried off Nell Cropsey from the start.

—Jim, son, wake up!

Mama was shaking me and the lamp was swinging in her other hand. I got that upset feeling from waking up too fast, till I realized it was Mama trying to get me up without disturbing my cousin that I was sharing the back bedroom with. But she was talking in a screech whisper like there was something wrong.

Fact was, I was a sound sleeper. Mama had to come after me several times every morning because when she'd call, I'd tell her I was getting up and then roll over back to sleep. But that night she shook me till I woke and there were dizzy-making shadows and her screech whisper.

—Jim, son, wake up! William Cropsey and his brother all down there with your daddy. They want to know where you left Nell.

—On the front porch of her house, I said. And I fell to sleep again when she left and closed the door. Or maybe not right to sleep. Maybe I heard some talk from downstairs or some noise when old man Cropsey and his brother went down off the porch and out to the street, scuffing on that hard frozen ground.

Lying here reminds me.

Then there was Chief Dawson with my daddy right behind him. I'd been sleeping faced away from the door, but when I woke again I turned and saw it weren't Mama this time but God now the law in there shaking me and saying,

—I want you to go over to Cropsey's with me, Jim.

I knew the Chief, course I did. He'd come into office in the election of '98. He was a Democrat and we were all Republicans and the Democrats cleaned up that year and my daddy got voted out of being county sheriff.

—All right, I said.

Hell, what was a little guy like me going to do? Go disagreeing with Chief Dawson, a big man and him the law? I got up and started dressing by the electric flashlight Chief carried. And I saw him take a good look at my blue steel pistol on the shelf.

Downstairs we met Officer Scarborough, who came along I guess in case I turned out to be some business. Two of em. What'd they think I'd done that they needed two of em to come get me?

It must of been an hour since old man Cropsey had come bothering me, and now Chief Dawson led me out into the cold and the bright moonlight. My jaw got tight and I forgot I'd been halfway warm for a bit up there in the bedroom, where my cousin was sleeping alone now and didn't know a damn thing about what all was happening.

He didn't know about Nell crying on her front porch, and he didn't know about the Cropsey men coming after me, or the law carting me over to where the same men were waiting to stare me down and blame me for things I never done.

The policemen rolled their bicycles and I walked between em, down Shepard Street to Charles Creek right where it flowed into the river. There was a wood bridge there then, a bridge that sat on a post and swiveled like a playing card with a pin through it to let the boats go by. A bridge keeper worked it, but if he was there that night he was asleep.

I was wide awake by then, and fast realizing I might be in some pretty deep trouble. When we got up near Pat Ives's house across the bridge I said,

—Here's where I met Len Owens earlier on, bout 11:30.

The Chief seemed to take in what I said, but he kept

Jim Wilcox

a stern face. Like that was his job what with Nell missing like this. It was past three in the morning.

—Jim, what do you make of this? Chief Dawson asked me, and I watched the words coming out of his mouth on the little breath clouds, because it was that cold and that bright from the November moon.

I didn't know what to think and I sure didn't know what to say, and I told em so.

—Where'd you last see Miss Cropsey?

We were going along the rivershore road, them rolling the cycles that rattled every so often on bumps and ruts, and if there was water standing in a place it was froze by then and maybe it crunched underfoot or if one of the cycles rolled over the ice just right.

—I left her standing on her porch, I said.

—Did she seem to be in any trouble? the Chief asked.

—She was crying when I left her.

—What about?

—I gave her back her picture and she said, I know what this means. We were a little on the outs.

—A little lovers' quarrel? Chief asked.

—She laughed at me, I said.

And she had laughed at me the night before, Tuesday night, after I'd brought her cousin Carrie back home from the roller skating rink. I stopped in the front hall on my way out to light a smoke and I overheard Carrie and Nellie and her sister Ollie laughing about how short I was. Why don't you call him Squatty? I'd heard Nellie say, and they all three laughed. I got out of the house before they knew I'd overheard.

She hadn't even spoken a word to me for two weeks— not a word.

—Why'd she laugh? asked the Chief.

I thought about earlier that same Tuesday night when

I come to pick Carrie up for the skating date and I'd asked Nellie how the corn on her foot was. But she wouldn't speak straight to me. She laughed then, too, and turned to her sister Ollie and said, All right. Nell Cropsey had been my girl for three-and-a-half years, almost since the day the Cropseys moved to Elizabeth City from Brooklyn, and now she wouldn't have anything to do with me or even talk to me, so I took Carrie out to spite her.

—Well, Chief, last night when I went in and asked her how her corn was she laughed at me. I told her the laugh would be on the other side.

We passed the shipyards on the river, where I'd been working back then. Up to the right and set back away from the river was Mr. John Fearing's big place where the Cropseys first stayed when they moved south in '98. They still stabled their horses there. I'd been in the stable with Carrie and Nell's sister Lettie the afternoon before, and I remembered thinking how much easier it was to breathe the stable air when it was cold like it was that November than in summer when it was either ripe or manure dusty in the air.

The first courting I did with Nell was out riding. Maybe I got the horse and rig from one of the downtown liveries or borrowed it—I don't know.

The sick old sandy-haired man Jim Wilcox, lying on his dirty bunk in the back room of Tuttle's garage, lying with a double-barrel twelve-gauge beside him, looked back through thirty-odd years of outlaw whiskey and prison and trials and couldn't recall just where he'd gotten the horse and buggy the first time he took Nell Cropsey out riding. But other things he did remember.

—Jim, did she ever speak of suicide?

I told the Chief it was mentioned tonight or last night one.

—How'd it come up?

—It come up, that's all. I don't know who brought it up.

We walked toward Cropsey's house all this while and I can hear those policemen's bicycles rattling still.

—Did Nell say anything about it? Chief Dawson asked.

—Yes, she said if she ever committed suicide she'd rather do it by freezing than any other way.

I saw the Chief was getting at the idea of Nellie killing herself cause I'd give back her pictures and left her crying on the porch. How could that of been my fault? She hadn't even been speaking to me. And she was planning to go to New York with her cousin Carrie on the next Saturday.

—Did she ever talk about suicide any other time?

—Yes, I said, a long time ago, when there was a crowd of us in the Cropsey summerhouse down by the river. She said if she was ever going to commit suicide she'd put a stone round her neck and do it well.

Chief Dawson and Officer Scarborough and I were almost to the Cropsey house then, and I looked down to where the summerhouse gazebo was, off to the left by the little beach where we'd used to go swimming or take the sailboat out from. The Cropsey house was easy to see across the old man's turnip patch, all lit up with oil lights inside and the bright moon outside.

How could I of known then how sorry I'd be, or how long it would all last? The policemen laid their bicycles up by the fence and went up that front walk just like I had for three years and more and then up the steps where I told em I left her crying. I never looked out on that river with her again.

Then Chief Dawson was knocking on the front door and it was opening and he was motioning me in. There was no way but to do it.

I was walking through the gates of hell thirty-three years ago if it was a day.

OLLIE CROPSEY

—Nell, can I see you out here a minute?

My sister didn't answer Jim Wilcox's question. I did. And the response I gave has trapped me in that moment I will live over and over till my dying day.

I was twenty then, and poor Nell was nineteen. She hadn't been speaking with Jim for a while, hoping I suppose that he would stop calling on her. She looked over at me for an answer, and I nodded as if to say yes, it was all right. Nell stepped out into the front hall with Jim. There was a brisk, cold draft because a large pane of glass was missing from the inner front door, so I got up and closed the dining room door behind her. That was the last I ever saw of my sister.

I let her go to speak with him because they had been awkward with each other long enough, on back into Indian summer and September of that year, 1901. Thanksgiving was a week and a day away, and Nell was leaving with Carrie the Saturday before to go north and spend it with Carrie's family at Stony Brook Farm in Rockland County, New York. It was time Nell and Jim settled it.

Perhaps if Papa had fixed the front hall door I wouldn't have been so quick about closing the dining room door and nothing would have happened to Nell.

Perhaps if he had replaced the missing pane with another piece of frosted, quilty-patterned glass . . .

Nell was so pretty. We have a tinted portrait of her, with her dark blue eyes and her chestnut hair. She always kept it tied back with a red ribbon. I've preferred to wear my hair up, after the fashions of Charles Dana Gibson. People used to bother me and tell me that the styles had changed, that I looked old-fashioned and queer. But what does it matter? I never leave the house anymore. I see no one but family. I know folks in Elizabeth City think I'm distracted and have thought it for years. It hurt me once, but now, what does it matter? I have a queasy stomach and take sick easily and have no wish to embarrass myself in public. So let the people of Elizabeth City talk as they will. Let the little girls come and try to catch a glimpse of me through the curtains because they've heard I'm a madwoman.

I will always dress in the Gibson fashion because it is a handsome way.

I will always grieve for Nellie.

After I closed the door behind her, I sat down and continued a conversation with my caller, Roy Crawford. That was five or ten minutes past eleven. We heard Nell's and Jim's steps out in the hall. Roy went on telling me some story or another, and I believe he might have gone on all night, but at half-past I interrupted him and told him it was time to go.

I couldn't understand Nell's staying out with Jim so long. She had scarcely looked at him all evening long.

—Don't get snappy, Roy said to me. Jim and Nell are out there yet.

I thought perhaps they had gone into the front parlor on the other side of the hall for a little more privacy and warmth than the hall allowed.

—I don't care if they are, Roy. You've got to make the first move, I said.

I worried that Papa might wake up and lose his temper. How many times over the years have I heard him say that he wished to God he hadn't stopped the townspeople from lynching Jim Wilcox when they came to our house with torches and ropes and asked him to lead their march to the jail?

—Well, there's no good being snappy, Roy said again. While he fetched his coat and hat, I put cups and saucers on the dining room table for Thursday's breakfast. When I finished, Roy rolled a cigaret and asked to be let out.

The vestibule door with its missing pane was open. The outside front door was open, too, and the screen door was loose and slapping back and forth in the wind. There was no sign of Nellie or Jim, so I thought he must have gone on home and that she was upstairs in bed. It was between 11:35 and 11:40 when Roy Crawford left our home.

I thought it odd, Nell's leaving me to shut up the house alone. I went upstairs to the front bedroom, the one above the sitting room, and spoke with Carrie, who was still awake. We looked out the large front window and watched Roy walking away in the moonlight toward town, till at last the small red glow from his cigaret vanished in the night. After a bit I went into the upstairs hall and sat unlacing my shoes by the lamp when I heard Papa rolling over and getting out of bed. Carrie's and my talking must have awakened him. I ran down to the back of the house, to the room over the kitchen which Nell and I shared.

She wasn't there.

I climbed into an empty bed at quarter to twelve and

lay there worrying. I could hear Papa rattling around in the kitchen below after going out to the privy. When the courthouse clock struck midnight, Nell still hadn't come in. Papa came upstairs just then, and shortly afterwards I fell asleep.

I had been in a doze for a bit, but I woke up hearing the dogs chasing toward the barn barking.

—Get your gun! Uncle Henry called to Papa from downstairs. I sat bolt upright and felt the bed for Nell. She still wasn't there and I ran out into the upstairs hall crying,

—Papa, don't shoot! Nell and Jim are down in the front hall yet! Then the whole house was awake and terribly upset and Nell was nowhere to be found.

We searched everywhere, under the house and around the house and all over it, but all we found was a parasol lying on the floor in the cold front hall. We were all crying. Papa told Mama not to worry, Nell had probably eloped with Jim Wilcox. He and Uncle Henry decided to go over to the Wilcox home and find out what had happened.

When they got back, Papa said he'd gone for Chief Dawson since all Jim would say was that he'd left Nell on the front porch. He and Uncle Henry kept searching and calling outdoors, tripping over the barking bird dogs. We watched from inside, trying to make them out in the moonlight.

Before too long there was a knock at the front door, and Chief Dawson brought Jim Wilcox in. Mama begged him to tell her where Nellie was. How could he not know? Jim took hold of one of the drapes and bunched it up in his left hand. Mama held him by the arm and said later that he was shaking.

—Jim, she begged him, for my sake and your mother's, tell me where Nell is.

He said he left her on the porch crying, that he'd told her to go in the house because she'd catch cold out there with so little on. He said he was going on over to town to meet some men and Nellie answered that she didn't care. Jim told Mama he could hear Nellie crying yet when he got to the front gate, eight or ten yards from the porch steps. He said it was a mystery to him.

I watched Jim Wilcox's hand shaking as he held the curtain and talked.

Chief Dawson left, promising to look into it in the morning when he could make out tracks on the ground outside if it were not frozen too hard for that.

Papa and Uncle Henry were halloing and crying out down by the rivershore, and once their calling stepped up so much we all thought Nell must have been found and rushed to the window to see. I could swear Jim hit his fist into his other hand right then. But it was a false alarm. Mama cried and said this just wasn't like Nell.

And it wasn't. I tried to remember back just a few hours, when Roy and I were talking, waiting for Nell to return. I hadn't heard a sound from Nell and Jim after those few steps in the hall, no sound except the wind blowing hard. It wasn't like Nell at all. She was timid—you couldn't get her to walk to the back steps without company.

They say that when the wind takes a mind to, it howls up the Pasquotank River like a banshee. I can hear it like that now, though we left that house we called Seven Pines in 1903, over thirty years ago. I hear that banshee wind and my closing the hall door behind Nell and Jim. I hear Roy's irritated remarks to me and the chinabell rattle of the cups against the saucers as I set the dining room table for a breakfast we never ate.

These details make up the moment which has become my life.

DENIAL

As hard as they asked and begged, just that hard he swore he didn't know, swore he knew no more than any of the rest there in the house by the Pasquotank River, bathed in moonlight. This was Nell's suitor and her only sweetheart since her family had moved south from Brooklyn, but he pled ignorance and offered no relief or hope or explanation.

—It's a mystery to me, Jim Wilcox said, and in so doing exacerbated the as yet unspoken fear that would go forth from the Cropsey house and engulf the town of Elizabeth City, drawing its people into an angry and desperate crusade to find the missing girl whom time and memory have honored: Beautiful Nell Cropsey.

SUSPICION

Jim Wilcox went home with the dawn that rolls into Elizabeth City from the sea beaches of Dare and Currituck, across the North River peach orchards, the potato fields row by row, the sorry-lot realm of the migrants. Almost as soon as he got home, Chief Dawson came and arrested him on general suspicion in the matter of Nell Cropsey's mysterious disappearance. Jim told his story again, how he left her crying on the porch, and it seemed that he was repeating the same small-change details over and over and he was getting tired of doing it. He finally wore out the Chief, who let him go on dog-tired to his job. By then it was near noon on Thursday, November 21st, 1901, and his girl had been missing for twelve hours.

In those days Jim worked over at Hayman's Marine Railways, one of the town's shipyard and drydock outfits that were booming since some Baltimore moneymen had reopened the Dismal Swamp Canal. The Pasquotank River through Elizabeth City was the southern entrance to the canal, which connected the Albemarle Sound with Norfolk and the Chesapeake Bay. Trade through town was up a quarter again over what it had been before the canal reopened in '99, and now there were machine shops and boatyards all along the waterfront.

Jim was one of a couple of dozen hands at Hayman's, and though he carried too much bulk on his 5'2" frame, Hayman said that Wilcox was a right strong bull considering his size. He never had trouble or did any slacking when it came to toting steel-heavy oak timbers about the boatworks. He also ran a small engine there, rigged for hauling boats of every size and condition up the railways into drydock for scraping and caulking and patching and refitting and painting. Hayman said Jim was strong and no slacker.

But he did have a reputation for combativeness and a vile temper. Folks recalled how he carried snakes and toads around in his pockets. He played baseball on one of the town teams and he was a member of a volunteer fire brigade, but he didn't have much in the way of friends. It didn't seem to bother him. He knew some people didn't like him because his family were Republicans. And then there was his uncle James Wilcox that Jim was named for, who had killed a man.

Jim Wilcox had scarcely gotten back to work at Hayman's shipyard when here came Chief Dawson early in the afternoon with a warrant for his arrest on the charge of abduction of Ella Maud Cropsey, sworn out against him by her father, William H. Cropsey. Jim would be coming, the Chief said, to a hearing that was being set up on the matter right then by Teddy Wilson, the big-eared, fat man Democrat mayor who was also a justice of the peace.

—I've told my part already, said Wilcox.

—Well, you'll tell it again, then, the Chief told him.

Word had begun to get around, and men packed into Mayor Wilson's offices to hear Jim and Mr. Cropsey and Ollie Cropsey all tell what had happened the night before.

People didn't believe Jim's saying that all he knew was what he was telling, that he had gone home to bed where Chief Dawson had later come and found him.

—Why did you leave her on the porch? they asked him.

—I told her to go on in, she'd catch cold if she didn't, Jim said.

—Why didn't you see her back to the door and see her safe inside? they asked.

—If I'd a known all this trouble was going to come of it, Jim Wilcox answered, I would have.

I would have.

By the time the hearing broke up on Thursday, November 21st, 1901, everyone in Elizabeth City over five years old was talking about the case of Nell Cropsey. Men who had filled Mayor Wilson's office went home disgruntled because Jim Wilcox, the ex-sheriff's boy, had been arrested twice and turned loose twice and the girl was still missing. They had talked to Jim Wilcox all night at the Cropsey house, all morning at the police station, all afternoon at the hearing, and there was no evidence that Jim Wilcox had done anything but leave a girl crying on a porch and go home to sleep.

Chief Dawson sent a wire off Thursday night to a man who lived in Suffolk, Virginia, on the far side of the Great Dismal Swamp. The man called himself a detective, and people said he owned the two best bloodhounds in the whole state of Virginia.

HURRICANE BRANCH

Out of the great swamp to Elizabeth City's north and east, way before the train's arrival in town, came its whistling and rumbling and echoing out of the wilderness, as if it were a stout log rolling slowly over a sheet of tin that was the sky, its rumbling soon become a roaring that seemed to come from everywhere at once.

They called it the Elizabeth City and Norfolk Railroad when the line opened in the early eighties, with the steam engine *W. G. Dominick* that could make the trip between the two towns in an hour. But once the line was extended west to Edenton on the Chowan River, the line's directors thought they ought to rename the road after the direction in which it was growing—so now they called it the Norfolk and Southern. The citizens of Elizabeth City fumed and blustered at having their town's name dropped from the railroad line, but the new name stood, and the cash rolled into Elizabeth City as more goods and produce rolled out. The town's population tripled between the coming of the railroad and the turn of the century. Elizabeth City prospered and forgave the railroad and got used to the rumble that echoed out of the swamp, signaling the approach of the train.

The depot and train yard sat beside the Pasquotank River's horseshoe bend, with a half-dozen sidings and a big wharf where railway agents dealt with the farm produce brought upriver, the profusion of vegetable baskets, boxes, and barrels come in by mothboat, sloop, and schooner, and with the goods bound south on the side-wheelers and lumber boats toward Albemarle Sound and the hundreds of creeks and glades along its periphery. The train yards were neat and handsome and all landscaped with bushes and willow trees whose long, tapering branches brushed the ground and the fence at the yard's edge along Pennsylvania Avenue beyond. Over sidings, switches, telegraph poles, stacks of ties, shovels, and crowbars, from early spring to late fall, the great swelling stream from the fields poured in.

By the time the morning train, the 11:40, had pulled to a stop on Friday, November 22d, 1901, a town crowd had already turned out, curious to see what sort of man their popular police chief had telegraphed off for and to see what sort of dogs that man would bring with him.

There was no mistaking any other Norfolk and Southern passenger for Hurricane Branch, who wore a blue-black wool uniform with small brass buttons. Across his front was a brace of pistols.

The citizens of Elizabeth City gave Hurricane Branch a hand as he stepped down off the train, and he smiled at the reception he was getting. Chief Dawson stepped forward to shake hands, and they walked together back to the baggage car. Hurricane Branch knocked on the big door till it rolled open and there was the baggage master holding a tether tied to two big bloodhounds. Branch made the throng back up and clear some space for his dogs and then got them down off the baggage car.

A boy turned to his friends, held his hands a foot or more apart, and said in wonder,

—They ears *that* long.

Hurricane Branch with his dogs and Chief Dawson and his town crowd began the mile-and-a-half trek over to the Cropsey house, their route following the horse-shoe bend of the Pasquotank, never more than several hundred yards away from the black river. Pennsylvania Avenue, thick with the piney planing-mill smells, turned into Poindexter Street and crossed Poindexter Creek bridge into one of the main business areas of the town. That was right by the Crystal Ice and Coal Company that blew up the previous July. But look at em now, somebody said, it takes em three wagons to handle all their trade.

Over the bridge there was Poindexter Street's amalgam of enterprises, including not only a host of dry goods, grocery, and confectionery shops, but also a marble works, a meat market, a cigar factory, a barber shop with a stuffed owl on a stand in the window, a fish market, Munden and Alexander's Awning Works, two bicycle shops, one of which also specialized in phonographs, White's Feed and Seed, the Chinese laundry, Crank's Bowling Alley, Walker's Millinery, and Tran Harris's bakery.

Branch's parade marched south past the shops, past the Cotton Club Dance Hall, on across Main Street, and gathered momentum as shop customers and keepers alike fell in with the excitement that two prize hounds were pulling through the heart of the river town. More came from the post office and joined, more still from the new turreted Citizens' Bank whose leafy shield high above the street pridefully said *1899*. Then by the old opera house, now fallen into disuse—more than one had wondered aloud about a theater built atop of an ice-house anyway.

And then, bearing left, Branch's parade crossed the Tiber Creek bog and mire with its pools of heavy green scum-covered stagnant water and the smell of sewage even in the cold November. Over the short bridge toward Dog Corner, where all hands at W. W. Griffin's Flour and Grist and Saw Mill, including Griffin himself, rushed to the doors and windows to gaze, not without awe, at the throng bearing down upon them.

—Let's go see can we help out, boys, said Griffin, and there was no more grinding that day.

And so on over the Charles Creek swivel bridge to what they called Dry Point, past Fowler's Net and Twine Mill and the collection of marine railways and the Kramer Sawmill. It was after noon as the crowd rambled down the rivershore road behind Hurricane Branch and the bloodhounds on their way to find Nell Cropsey.

Jim Wilcox was sitting on a fence there by Hayman's shipyard when the crowd passed by. His girlfriend Nell Cropsey had been missing over a day and a half, but of all those who put down their labors to join in zealous search, Jim Wilcox was not one.

The citizens' army led by Hurricane Branch and Chief Dawson marched past Wilcox and on to the Cropsey house farther down the rivershore road. They stopped and waited at the fence out front. Chief Dawson recalled later that a couple hundred or so had turned out, but somebody else could have sworn that by the time William H. Cropsey stepped onto his wide front porch, there were two bloodhounds and fifteen hundred people that had all come looking for Beautiful Nell Cropsey.

Across the front of the house were two porches: an unbroken railing ran along the upper porch, and there were a half-dozen steps in the middle of the lower. A lumberman named Preyer had built the place in 1891, and they say he took the best logs as they came to him, pulled them out, and saved them for this house. In the very front and center of the house there was a cupola tower with a sharp-rise pyramidal roof. One's eyes immediately leapt to this decorative tower, and the mind in tow just a moment behind responded—the Cropseys live in a clapboard castle.

Hurricane Branch took it all in. A man, his wife, his brother, his niece, and his nine children were living in the house they called Seven Pines. Why had this man Cropsey, from an established family in a city like Brooklyn, moved this huge family south to a little river town right when several of his daughters were of marrying age? Didn't he have a pretty good job up north?

—Excise commissioner for New Utrecht, said Chief Dawson.

Cropsey came south to this place to farm and trade, because (the commercial circulars said) the low tidewater and sound country was a garden spot. Just scratch the surface of its soil and the land would embarrass with the riches it could grow. Turn the rich soil and the blue clay and the lime marl and the rot of embedded shells, raise it to the surface, and the fertility would embarrass.

The girl Nell Cropsey was to have gone north with her cousin for Thanksgiving and part of the winter, Chief Dawson told Branch. She was supposed to have left tomorrow, Saturday the twenty-third of November.

Hurricane Branch took it all in: there were bushes about the house grounds, utility stairs and a small dou-

Seven Pines, the Cropsey home

ble porch around at the back of the west side, broad panes of glass in the front windows. It had been a bright night by the moon, and she had come out onto this dark porch and disappeared.

—People don't send for me less there's trouble, Branch said to William Cropsey. Cropsey, taciturn and not given to any appreciation of attention drawn to himself, looked over the crowd, which though not unruly was pressing at his fence as men shuffled and craned their necks. At his glance many dropped their eyes.

—Always work with such an audience, Mr. Branch? Cropsey gestured.

—Folks like to see these dogs work. Most times hounds are out it's convicts at night. Nobody's going to turn out for convicts at night, but this, *this* is different, Branch said. Could you get me some of Miss Cropsey's socks or stockings?

Dawson and Branch spoke low while Cropsey went inside, talking about how the crowd could ruin the attempt at tracking the lost girl, how a criminal investigation could turn into a carnival event, and then Branch had a few words for the crowd.

—Good people. Good people, this is Hurricane Branch speaking, he began from the porch steps, like any stump politician. He warned them about his dogs not exactly being house pets, how they could get nervous if anybody disturbed them while they were working, they got that intense. How the Chief would deal with anybody planning to get in the way, cut up or carry on, because there was a young lady missing and this was serious business.

William Cropsey returned with a pair of Nell Cropsey's shoes and stockings and held them out to Hurricane Branch.

—Will these do?

—Do just fine, Branch said. He put the shoes and stockings to his hounds' noses and dropped them on the porch floor. He let them get worked up and snuffling.

—Looka here, Tiger, Sampson. Looka here.

The crowd was transfixed.

Branch had pulled the tether up tight so that he was standing right over the hounds when they had enough scent from the shoes and were ready to go on it.

—All right, yelled Hurricane Branch, and they were off down the front steps and the path with the hounds going steadily and snuffling through the wide gate and through a parting in the crowd and continuing apace across the road to the summerhouse at the river's edge. They went in and around the gazebo several times before the one called Tiger tugged back toward the big house. Branch let the tether out and the hounds pulled him toward the fence some ten yards or so to the west or town side of the front gate. Chief Dawson held the tether line as the hounds went under the low slat of the fence and Branch climbed over top. They cut across Cropsey's turnip patch till some fifty yards along that path the bloodhounds stopped and turned back again in the direction of the Pasquotank River. There was a gasp, a collective, involuntary *Oh!* from the slack-jawed mob.

The flamboyant Branch followed his hounds on their beeline to a short gate in the fence some two hundred fifty yards from the Cropsey porch. He stayed right with them. Through the short gate without slackening they followed that track across the rivershore road and onto a pier that ran a couple hundred feet out into the river.

At the end of that pier they stopped.

These were the finest sleuth hounds in Virginia.

—We'll try it again, Branch said coolly and traipsed

through the crowd with the snuffling hounds to start over with the lost girl's shoes and socks at the front porch. And again the hounds ambled down to the river, then cut back across the turnip patch, turned and smelled their way to the end of the pier, and so on all afternoon, till the dark started coming on and the townspeople had had enough of the dog chase and carnival, and the hounds were tired and confused from the tramping of the mob and could no longer make track beyond the porch. The excitement was over, and the mob broke down into small knots of men staring out at the black river and pointing at the summerhouse, the turnip patch, and the pier and talking with morbid speculation.

Hurricane Branch fed and watered his bloodhounds Tiger and Sampson while Chief Dawson went to tell William Cropsey what they would do next. They would search the houses, especially in the Negro district, and the businesses. Search the town, sure, on the slim chance she was hiding or somebody was keeping her.

After that, only one thing left to do.

DRAGGING THE RIVER

The Pasquotank, one of five rivers that rise and flow unnaturally out of the morass of the Great Dismal Swamp, meanders its dark serpentine way from South Mills, where the canal locks were, on to Camden the courthouse crossroads, and then the last four slow, rolling miles down to the Narrows at Elizabeth City. There round that horseshoe bend it fans out wide—the *Pask-e-'tan-ki* of the Tuscarora and the Croatan, a black, murky, pungent river.

It was November 1901, and a cold snap had set hard

upon the little river town. Saturday, November 23d, was the day the missing girl was supposed to have taken the Old Dominion steamer up the Chesapeake with her cousin Carrie on their way north. Instead it was the day when townsmen came out in their skiffs and dories and sharpies and beneath a platinum sky began dragging the Pasquotank for her body.

Others watched from among the rust-gold cypresses and tall pines along shore while the men in boats threw the draglines out. Time and again the grapnel flukes snagged and the lines tightened and, with apprehension, other men in other boats stopped and looked to see if they were bringing her up. But it would just be some muck-covered stump or cast-off debris from the mills.

They looked for Nell Cropsey in this black river.

Its water was dark from tannic-acid leachings of the juniper trees along the rivershore back up toward the headwaters, and those leachings were preservative—the dark, discolored water wouldn't go bad and had often filled the water casks of ocean-bound ships, had even gone along with Admiral Perry to Japan fifty years before.

It was a gruesome business, and as on the day before with Hurricane Branch and his dogs, the crowds on shore thinned as the work of the drag boats became routine and seemed destined to fail. A few knots of onlookers and speculators remained, and there was talk.

—She ain't in that river, they said.

—Somebody carried her away by boat, they said.

—Somebody carried her off and they're holding her for ransom. I heard her uncle's a big judge up in New York—she's worth good money live.

Rumor grew into theory and theory into purported fact. There was no shame that morbid curiosity could not quash. No one in the community tired of retelling and refiguring the case of Nell Cropsey, and every hour that elapsed upped the emotional ante.

—Anything could have happened, they said. She could be anywhere.

Jim Wilcox did not work on the drag boats, but he watched and was watched. Once, when the draglines tightened, they thought they really had her this time, and a fellow named Davenport was standing near Jim on shore.

—It was right opposite the old brickyard, Davenport said, and I had been hearing so much talk that when I saw something coming up I looked at Jim very straight and I thought I saw his face turn pale.

JIM WILCOX

I got off the Southern eastbound in Raleigh a few days before Christmas 1918. Four newspapermen come walking up to me out of the steam fog from the train brakes.

—How's it feel?

—What'd you tell the governor?

—Going home for Christmas?

I was coming in from the prison farm up in the mountains where I'd been when I got word about the pardon.

I was a trusty and they'd never locked me up. They didn't have to. I heard em say that never in the history of the North Carolina prisons had there been a perfect record like mine with not one black spot against it.

I'd started pulling my time at Central Pen in Raleigh in 1903. Once while I was there the lighting system broke down so I sent word to the warden to let me try and fix it. I did, too. And that phrenologist who come through testing prisoners said I'd of been a great engineer if I'd got proper training. Another Edison. Later they sent me on up to the mountains.

I heard how my poor mama went door to door back in Elizabeth City looking to get signatures on her petitions to the governor to get me out. People didn't answer their doors or else they sent their colored help to say they was gone and they was sorry, Missus Wilcox. Mama went through it anyway but twice Governor Craig turned me down. If I'd had any chance for a pardon it sure got shot to hell when Nell's mother wrote the governor and talked against me like she and all the rest of the Cropseys have ever since Nell disappeared.

When Mama was dying she wrote me from her deathbed saying please Jim and begging me to tell her the truth about Nell Cropsey cause she had to know before she died. I wrote her right back the truth was I was innocent as a baby, and before she passed on she sent me a Bible. I kept a lock of Nell's hair inside it, and I had her picture on my wall. During the Great War I come down with the TB and they said I weren't going to make it. I told this one prisoner there with me that I couldn't go to my Maker with a lie on my lips, so help me God. I called him over to what they said was going to be my deathbed and told him I wanted the world to know I was not guilty of the crime for which I stood accused and convicted.

Well, I pulled through after all, but I never could shake this cough.

Captain Peoples come to see me when I was better. He was the prison superintendent and he knew me all the time I'd been sent up. He wanted me to write the new governor, Bickett, who he said would listen to my case and understand it. He said Governor Bickett was a good man who paid attention to the plight of the prisoners and

that he was catching hell in the papers because he reviewed so many cases and turned so many men loose
that he thought had pulled enough time. They said in
the papers that he was running a pardon mill down at
the governor's mansion. That's what Captain Peoples
told me.

I was a model prisoner.

I tried to help out back when Nell was first missing
and everybody turned against me. Daddy sent for Deputy Charlie Reid to come and carry me over to the Cropseys' and clear things up between me and them about
Nell. Right after she was first gone.

I was around on the back porch and I heard Deputy
Reid's knocking and went and let him in. He talked with
Mama and Daddy a while and Mama was crying. Daddy
said he wanted the whole town to know that Wilcoxes
didn't buck the law and Deputy Reid would be there to
witness.

I set out with him and I was nervous about it but I
had to do it. Before we'd even got to the Charles Creek
bridge, he dug into me and told me I oughta talk.

—If you know anything, Jim, in justice to your family
you ought to let it be known.

I held my temper best I could and thought about how
tired I was getting of nobody believing me when I said I
told all I knew, but before I said a word Deputy Reid
spoke again.

—Looks to me you ought to explain this whole thing,
Jim, as it's getting you in trouble. Not just for your sake
but for your mother's sake too.

It broke her heart, I know, for me to be in such a
scrape and no way out unless Nell Cropsey just showed
up. People had it in for me from the start.

—I've told all I can tell, I said.

Well, Captain Peoples wrote a letter to the governor and showed it to me. He told Governor Bickett that it was the first time in eighteen years with the prison system he'd ever appealed to a governor on a prisoner's behalf, but that he'd known me for fifteen years and my record was perfect so he was appealing for mercy for me.

So when I had recovered enough from the TB, I sat down and wrote:

Dear Governor Bickett:

For sixteen years and over I have been unjustly punished and now broken in spirit and health I come to you asking mercy. I too can see that the circumstances are against me for it is a very mixed up affair but I do not know any more about the affair than an unborn babe. For fifteen years and seven months I have worked hard and faithful, a record few men ever attain, fifteen years with nothing against it. My mother and father have been taken away during that time. Do you not think I have been punished enough? I ask you to please pardon me and let me spend my last days with what is left of my loved ones.

We put the two letters in an envelope together and sent them off to the governor.

It was December 1918, and the war was over.

Governor Bickett made a special trip to the prison farm to see me and spent the afternoon talking with me alone. He told me that people back in Pasquotank had come around and many had written letters saying they were satisfied I'd been punished enough, that I should be let go. And there were more who thought me innocent and were finally willing to come out and say so. Solicitor Ward who'd become a judge—he wrote Governor Bickett six months before he died asking mercy for me.

The telegram arrived December 20th, 1918, saying the Governor granted me full pardon and I was free to go home.

Captain Peoples helped me get ready. He gave me a Kodak and the best clothes we could find round the prison farm off there in the middle of nowhere. I got me a brown suit and a army shirt and a red tie for a belt and I wore my high hunting boots. Oh, and my slouch hat with the special hatband that was the skin of an eleven-rattle rattler I'd killed up there. I shaved except for my mustache and the captain got the four-in-hand supply rig ready for me and somebody to drive me in. We shook hands and said good-bye and I was off to catch the next Southern east.

The newspapermen come at me on the platform there at the Raleigh station and I told em finally somebody believed I was innocent, and I was awful glad it was the governor. I rolled a cigaret and waited there for the state carriage to come carry me down to spend the night at Central Pen. The next day they'd give me a certified copy of my pardon and then I'd pull out.

That carriage didn't come and didn't come and those newsmen got to making me nervous so I figured I'd duck em. I said I was sorry but I was going to wait in a café near there till the carriage came. But they just followed me in and it was like they were closing in on me. I rolled a cigaret and they stared at the way I struck a light between my thumb and pointing finger.

—How bout a picture, Jim? one of em said.

That called my mind to those photographers from the Chicago papers back at the trial in 1902. I'd had enough pictures of me took back then. So I pulled out that Kodak Captain Peoples gave me and told em joking like to watch out I'd shoot *them* if they weren't careful.

—Come on, Jim, just one picture.

I told em I'd pose for one down at the newspaper office but not there in the café that night. I'd been traveling all day and I was tired and those newsboys made me nervous. I told em I'd be around Raleigh for a day or two but I knew I wouldn't.

I won't broke, not me. Had some money on me from selling leatherwork and carved canes I'd made when I was in prison. I got my pardon and the hell with the newsboys. I just dropped out of sight for a few days, figuring I'd lay low and just plain let the dust settle a bit fore I went home.

I caught the morning train out of Norfolk on Christmas Eve 1918, and it was late, nearly two in the afternoon, when it pulled into the new station out at the far end of Main Street. I remember the red curvetile roof, and my sisters Sadie and Annie Mae, and a good bunch of others waiting for the train.

—Where've you been, Jim?

—We've met every train. We've been wild worrying.

—We got no word from you.

They were both crying, and I guess I was too. I was back home free and pardoned after sixteen years being sent up. I told em I was glad to be home.

A young woman I didn't recognize spoke to me there and said she was Josh Dawson's girl, did I remember her?

Lord have mercy.

This was what had become of Josh's little three-year-old Evelyn that he'd brought by the Elizabeth City jail to say good-bye before I went off to Central Pen in 1903. The guard closed the cell door behind Josh and his little girl and when it slammed she looked so frightened I picked her up and set her on my knee.

—Don't you worry now, I told her. You haven't done anything wrong. You're not in any trouble, child.

And there she was when I come home in 1918, grown up and saying, Here, Mister Jimmy, this is my husband John Tuttle, and then they were off in a hurry to get on the train. Going over to Hertford to spend Christmas with her husband's folks.

The train pulled out and the steam fog swirled round the new station. I remember thinking the Tuttles were nice to me and I'd go see em after they got back from the holiday. Never thought I'd be begging them to put me up like this, but here I am.

Here I am.

OLLIE CROPSEY

Papa had gone out the Sunday afternoon after Nell was lost. He went down to one of the shipyard piers to look for her. Not a word from her and by then the papers were starting to take it up. Papa told us there was going to be a town meeting about it.

When he came back from the piers I was surprised because he had brought Jim Wilcox back with him. A colored boy had run up to Papa out on the pier and said Deputy Reid wanted a word with him in the shipyard office. Papa walked over and heard a tap on the office window and Deputy Reid was motioning him in. He had Jim inside with him. They talked a bit but Jim wouldn't cooperate. He didn't even want to come over to our place and face Mama, and Papa just about had to make him.

One of my sisters and I were sitting in the living room when they arrived. Everyone was cold and stiff and Jim was no comfort at all. When Mama walked in she went straight to Jim and put her hand on his shoulder.

—Please tell me where Nell is, she said.

—I can't tell you anything about where she is, Jim said.

—You left her crying? Mama asked.

—Yes.

—What was she crying about?

—I told her I was going to quit her, Jim said.

It was quiet then for a moment.

—Had you ever seen Nell cry before, Jim?

He said yes, he had, back in October during the big church meetings when the evangelist came to town. I had already heard them arguing then and I knew they were falling out. Carrie, our cousin, had just come for a visit from Brooklyn with Uncle Andrew, who was a judge there. Jim said he had told her back then that he was going to quit seeing her, and she had cried.

—I don't believe it, Jim, Mama shook her head. I just don't believe it.

Deputy Reid spoke up and asked me to show him how it had been the night when she disappeared. I walked into the dining room, which was just behind the living room on the same side of the house, and the deputy followed me.

—That's where I sat, I said and pointed to a chair. I showed him where Jim had sat in the little rocker between the corner stove and the door to the hall. Then I stepped into the front hall just like Jim had and peeked back in and said,

—Nell, can I see you out here a minute? Just as he had.

We all went out on the front porch and Deputy Reid asked Jim to please show where Nell was standing and in what position. Jim went to the right side of the piazza, put his right hand up on the porch post there, and leaned the right side of his head against his hand. That's how she was, Jim said, leaning against the post like this and crying.

—Where were you? asked the deputy.

Jim stood on the second porch step. He said he told Nell twice to go into the house to keep from catching cold. He lit a cigaret and told her again to go in, that he was going to meet some men in town, but she kept crying and said, I don't care. Go on. So he left her and headed for town after being out there for ten or fifteen minutes altogether. He said that was all he could remember.

Then Jim and Deputy Reid left.

Mama was crying and saying she didn't believe Jim at all and how could he be so?

I shivered to remember the postcard Mama had written her mother in Brooklyn just two days before Nell disappeared, saying

I have lost all fear of the number thirteen. For more than a month we have sat down to table, thirteen of us —Will, our nine children, Carrie, my brother Henry, and I. And there is no indication of the ill luck that is supposed to follow the unlucky number.

Now every morning Mama was walking all down by the river, by the summerhouse, and every evening, too. She spent the rest of the time sitting upstairs staring out her bedroom window or up in the cupola tower keeping her vigil for Nell. And I wondered why, oh, why, Lord, had I let her leave the house with Jim Wilcox?

Town Meeting

On Saturday night, November 23d, 1901, the local telephone operator called every preacher in Elizabeth City and asked would the preacher mind announcing in church Sunday morning that there was going to be a meeting that night at the Academy of Music. She had been put up to it by some prominent townsmen.

A few well-placed words from the pulpits, and seven hundred men filled the downtown theater to find out what was going on about Nell Cropsey.

What was being done?

The theater occupied the upper rear of the Bee Hive One Price department store building, which had gone up in the late nineties on the northwest corner of Main and Poindexter. The store took up the whole ground floor; there were offices in the second floor front, and a small ballroom above them. Lawyer Ed Aydlett worked out of there. The theater itself was one of those that in a few years would be called a vaudeville house.

Vaudeville was a nascent form, child of *commedia*, minstrel show, operetta, and melodrama, being born to troupe with sets, costumery, innumerable hats, masks, and disguises, to troupe by whatever means of transport could get the players to the next town that could boast a palace as plainly grand as the Academy of Music in Elizabeth City, North Carolina. It had a swooping balcony, half a dozen fat black heat stoves down each side wall, and a small proscenium stage with a fluted gold column on each side to frame the action that vaulted forth from or fell flat upon the boards once the great velours were pulled apart.

But tonight's drama was dead serious.

There was a wild alarm over the girl who had been

missing without a trace for four days now, and seven hundred men crowded the Academy to see and hear it all for themselves.

—Funds should be raised to clear the mystery, said Professor Hinton, the balding, bearded schoolmaster.

—We must appoint a committee of men who are not tied down to any party or faction in town, said Harry Greenleaf, the hardboiled civil engineer. Men who will go ahead fearlessly and regardless of who may be hurt and bring this crime home to the man responsible for it.

There was frequent applause.

—I want this committee to go to work unfettered in any way, said lawyer Ike Meekins, the town's former Republican mayor. If they so decide then I am willing to see the money I contributed spent on tar and feathers. We must sift this crime to the bottom and find out who carried this girl away.

The local board of commissioners had already established a two hundred dollar reward for evidence with which to convict the murderer or abductor of Nell Cropsey, and a hundred dollars to whoever found her dead or alive. Now the citizenry at large was funding a full-scale search.

Hats passed through the crowd. Hands reached deep into pockets, and those without cash or coin wrote pledges on whatever paper scraps were handy. Contributions ranged from twenty-five cents to twenty-five dollars, and in just a few minutes' time the report came from the stage that two hundred thirty dollars had been collected to fund the work of a citizens' committee.

All of a sudden the law was in the hands of everyone and no one.

They were a vigilante force, and they chose Harry Greenleaf to lead them. They didn't particularly like him, but he was well known and he was respected. Greenleaf was one of those who had come down from the north to help open up the Albemarle to the world, and by now he had lived in Elizabeth City for twenty-eight years. He had surveyed the Elizabeth City and Norfolk Railway in 1876–77, and he had led the gandy dancers in building yet another railway between Mackey's Ferry and Belhaven down below the Albemarle Sound. And he spent a month back in the Great Dismal Swamp fixing Colonel Byrd's hundred-and-fifty-year-old boundary between Virginia and Carolina. He was head of the Alligator Lumber Mills in Dare County, and he had been involved in running the Camden Telephone line from Elizabeth City to Norfolk.

Harry Greenleaf lived right next door to the courthouse in a big white house with columns and a front porch. He wasn't particularly popular with these people, but he had done a lot for their town. He would lead them, and they would get to the bottom of the matter.

So several hundreds of men who bonded elsewhere as Masons, Odd Fellows, Knights, or Woodmen, in secret society realms of prophets, regents, wizards, dictators, had now created from their number another special society, a Committee of Five, not tied to the old codes and traditions of medieval burial societies but dealing instead with a real mystery, with secrets perhaps unfathomable. And there were real and growing fears about what they might find and have to do, for this whole affair of Nell Cropsey and Jim Wilcox had caught them off guard and pervaded their town with a fearful confusion.

From the same stage where Charles C. Vaught's Comedy Company, featuring Miss Tucker and a clever band of comedians, had just completed a three-night stand,

and with the blessing of the town's business and political leaders, this vigilante outfit self-invested as the Committee of Five began its work.

JUDGE ANDREW CROPSEY

He was an important man and one of the Old Dutch Brooklyn Cropseys, so the *New York Journal and American* sent a writer down to Judge Cropsey's office at Number Three Chambers Street in New York when they got word his niece was missing.

The Judge's daughter Carrie had written him the morning after Nell's strange disappearance, and the letter reached his Blythebourne home Saturday. He had telegraphed immediately for particulars and got a special delivery response from his brother William on Monday morning, November 25th. Nell Cropsey was still missing as of Saturday, the message said. The whole country round was stirred up and there was talk of lynching Jim Wilcox. The Judge wired again, and the reply came right back early Monday afternoon—still no trace of Nell.

—It's the strangest thing I've ever heard of, Judge Cropsey told the *Journal* man.

—I know my niece very well. She'd never consent to an elopement, nor would she take her own life. In her letter, Carrie says the impression of the family is that Nell was seized, carried off into a boat, possibly thrown in the river or held captive perhaps in the Dismal Swamp—the suggestion is maddening to those who love her. Nell and Carrie were to have left on an Old Dominion Line steamer Saturday last to come up for a family Thanksgiving. And I understand that two young men, old friends of the family, were to come up on the same steamer—I see no reason for publishing their names, said the Judge.

More than the papers were interested. Letters and wires flooded the Judge's home and the homes of the many other Cropsey relatives who lived about Brooklyn.

—What do you hear of Nell?

—How can we help?

—The Lord will guide this lamb safely back to the flock.

—Who would harm her?

—Our prayers are with you.

—Our prayers are with you.

Then came two more alarming telegrams from the North Carolina Cropseys. From his brother:

Nell not found. Ascertain the cost of sending a good detective here from New York. Important. Wire immediately.

W. H. Cropsey

and from his niece, Alletta, one of Nell and Ollie's older sisters:

Have not had one word of poor Nell yet. Have made a most careful search for her without result. Will let you know as soon as we hear anything. We are almost wild.

Lettie

What could the Judge do? He had taken Carrie down to that river town in Indian summer for a long visit with her cousins, and now this. He had planned for a cheerful Thanksgiving reunion at their Rockland County farm, and now this.

—There's a strong suspicion of Wilcox, I hear, Judge Cropsey told the *Journal* man. Those young Southerners are hotheaded fellows and there's no telling what they would do in an emergency where love is at stake.

OLLIE CROPSEY

I tried to comfort Mama. We all made an effort to believe Nell was still alive, but it was no easy task with the boats dragging the river, back and forth, day after day, just offshore in front of our house.

Every thought about what might have become of my sister was horrible. Papa thought Nell was alive but where, he had no notion. Chief Dawson had searched a hundred of the colored houses in southwest Elizabeth City garret to cellar with no luck. He said he thought poor Nell had been murdered and that whoever had done it carried her downriver in a boat and threw her overboard out of range of the search.

Suicide was mentioned.

Nell was about to embark on a long winter's trip to Brooklyn, our ancestral home. She and Carrie had been very popular students together at Pratt Institute, and they were full of anticipation over their journey home. Nell and Jim were on the outs, but that was from *her* side, not his. She wanted to be rid of him—I could never seriously consider the idea that my sister Nell would have killed herself over Jim Wilcox. A writer from the Charlotte newspaper called at our home during the search and I spoke with him, told him there was no reason for Nell to have thought of either suicide or eloping with Jim Wilcox.

—I have no suspicion of intimacy between Nell and Jim, I said. They put it on the front page.

In my heart I thought Jim had hidden Nell somewhere because during the search he would walk by

Seven Pines, our home, carrying bags of groceries and grinning up at the house as if he wanted us to know he was taking food to Nell wherever he was keeping her.

Either he really was or he wanted us to *think* so—he was that cruel.

My little sister Caroline was only a few years old when Jim courted Nell, but she always said she could remember that Jim was mean to our cats and sometimes pinched her on the back of her legs. She was so frightened of him that when Governor Bickett pardoned him, Caroline insisted that her husband move their family away. She told me she was afraid Jim Wilcox would come back and get her like he got Nell.

We were all frightened of him.

After Nell had been missing for a week, the searchers brought out an old iron cannon that Papa said was probably left over from the Civil War when the federal gunboats sailed upriver and shelled and occupied Elizabeth City. They set the old cannon on the rivershore and fired it over and over out across the Pasquotank River, trying to raise Nell's body to the surface by percussion.

Papa said the men were complaining that the dragging equipment was inadequate and that the draglines mostly had small fishhooks not designed to grapple a body. Lord, I thought, if Nell were in that black river and they should hook her!

They seemed to try everything and still never find her, so we kept hoping. They even tried putting quicksilver in a bread loaf, believing it might float to the spot in the river where Nell's body lay. They threw sticks of dynamite into the river from the drag boats.

I winced as the shore by Seven Pines rocked with one explosion after another.

And I winced at what turned up in the papers. A fortune teller in Norfolk was saying Nell had been taken away by boat and was alive and engaged to be married. Deputy Reid, who later became our sheriff, was scoffing at a rumor that Jim had paid someone to carry Nell away.

I kept up with these reports and grieved. And I climbed the stairs to the cupola tower where Mama kept her vigil and tried to be some comfort to her. What had ever let me nod yes to Nell and let her go?

JUDGE ANDREW CROPSEY

It was the first of December, 1901, when Judge Cropsey in New York opened the letter that read:

I am only a poor workingman but I am honest. As I was going out of town the night your niece disappeared, I was astonished to hear a remark followed by many threats. I judged there were in the party two, but to my astonishment, there was only one. As I was not fifteen yards away from the person, that was about four hundred yards away from the house, and the time was 11:45 p.m. Be sure that I am not giving you any wild talk, but the truth as I think the man who deserves punishment ought to be locked up. The night I refer to, I was not 400 yards away from your brother's residence, and I know more than some people think I do.

Desperately yours,
George Hellenback

More information was to be had if the Judge would wire or write Hellenback in care of

General Delivery
The Bourse Building
Philadelphia, Pennsylvania

Instead, he wired Chief Dawson in Elizabeth City, who found a lodging record indicating that a man with a similar-sounding name, one A. E. Wellenbeck of New Milford, New Jersey, had been in town on November 19th and 20th. Wellenbeck turned out to be a drummer for the New York Molasses Company, and he denied being in Elizabeth City as well as all knowledge of the case. The Philadelphia address proved a dead end.

Judge Cropsey found and employed a detective named Connor, who promptly headed south to join the search.

JIM WILCOX

I was minding my own business working there at the shipyard in early December '01, when along come Chief Dawson and arrested me again and hauled me off to the courthouse downtown for a second hearing.

There was a howling mob followed me and the Chief all the way. My daddy, when he heard about it, went and got Lawyer Aydlett to speak for me in court. After all, we'd hired him before when my uncle was on trial for killing the pollkeeper down at Newbegun. Aydlett was the biggest damn Democrat in these parts and we Wilcoxes were Republicans, but we hired him because he was good.

Lawyer Aydlett weren't much of a speaker, but he was tough—he hit hard and didn't ask no quarter. He took my case right into that second hearing and I listened while people talked about me and how I acted and then

I really began to get the drift of what people were thinking and saying.

They were after me from the start.

—Jim's a bit cold and aloof, lawyer Aydlett told the court, but that's just the way he is by nature. He and his father—you all know Tom Wilcox, used to be sheriff. Lawyer Aydlett smiled a bit about that because he'd helped beat my daddy out of office. Anyway, Aydlett said, Jim and his daddy are no less concerned than anyone in town for the welfare of Miss Cropsey.

I sat there and listened to old man Cropsey saying how I weren't myself that night. He said I looked at my watch a lot and was absorbed in some faraway proposition. Well, Mr. Cropsey went up to bed almost as soon as I got there to Nell's that night. I'd like to know how he knew those things when he weren't even downstairs with us, unless Ollie told him. If I could of just had ten minutes with Ollie I know I could straighten this whole thing out. I've tried since I come home from prison but they won't let me see her. They keep her locked up in that house out on Southern Avenue.

Cropsey told that hearing that my behavior since Nell disappeared was indifferent, that I didn't care to search for where she was because I already knew.

Fanny Mitchell and Alex Brown swore they saw me talking with two men near the corner of South Road Street and Shepard Street just before midnight the night Nellie disappeared. They said they'd seen me talking there in the cold, bright night and that I'd split off from the two men and walked back down Shepard Street to my house.

Hell, I told em I'd left Nell on the porch when I headed for town to meet some men. I told that part, didn't I?

Lawyer Aydlett told the court I had no idea where

Nell was and that me and my daddy would do anything we could to help out but the Cropseys never asked for any help from us, no sir.

They let me go on a thousand dollar bail and a promise that I'd report to Mayor Wilson's office every day at noon so the town could keep tabs on me. That hearing went on five hours and I was tireder when I left than if I'd of been toting timbers round Hayman's shipyard. Some New York newsman caught me on Main Street outside and asked me what I really thought became of Nell.

Want to know what I really thought?

—I don't think what happened between us would of made Nell kill herself, I told him. Not at first, but I been thinking that suicide by freezing might be her fate since she'd made remarks in that direction.

—By freezing? he asked like I was crazy. He said his paper sent him south on account of the Cropseys being a big deal family back in New York.

I told him once a suicide discussion had come up by my telling a story about how I nearly met with a buggy accident and how I'd said I wouldn't of cared if I'd been ground to pieces between the wheel and the vehicle it was so cold and freezing hard and there was ice on the ponds the next morning.

When I got back to Hayman's shipyard, Mr. Hayman come up to me and said he wished to the Lord they could find Miss Nell.

—I wish to the Lord they could too, Mister Hayman, I said. I'd go help look for her, but what if I found her? They'd say right away I was the one killed her and knowed where her body was all along.

—What makes you so sure she's dead, Jim? he said.

Next morning when I was coming in to work, Mr. Hayman met me and fired me. He told me I was discharged from my job till I could establish my innocence in the matter. Now how was I supposed to do that?

I was walking back to town on the Camden causeway one day while she was missing, and M. G. Morrissette gave me a ride in his wagon. After a ways I saw he kept looking at me and I realized he'd seen my pistol with the taped handle that I had stuck in my waist.

—What're you doing with that, Jim?

—None of your business, and if you ever tell anyone you saw it I'll blow your goddamn brains out.

I was glad for the ride but that needling made me mad. Way things were going for me, I had to protect myself, and I didn't want word getting around and folks jumping to wrong conclusions like so many already had.

I tried to keep in good spirits and sorta hung around town and checked in to the mayor's, but people were down on me, avoiding me and all like that. I asked my daddy what I oughta do, and he got me a permit to go down Newbegun way to do some hunting and stay clear of this mess for a while.

The whole town had it in for me from the beginning, and I knew it.

THE CLAIRVOYANT

—Wilcox killed Ella Cropsey. He had an accomplice. The girl was chloroformed, wrapped in a big blanket, placed in a Dayton wagon, and driven back into the country where she was killed and thrown into a deep well by an old house, said the clairvoyant.

She was Madam Snell Newman, the famous spiritualist from Norfolk, and she told the papers what she thought had occurred.

Harry Greenleaf and his Committee of Five read the story and brought her down from Norfolk to see what she might be able to divine about the case right there on the spot.

Was she a gypsy? People in town talked about the strange old world-ramblers with odd accents and exotic women and children with dark eyes and dark hair and dark skin, and their wagons with pots rattling off the sides. They read palms and tea leaves and knew the stars in the sky. They stole children. There was an old warning to children: Get up on the porch or crawl under it, there's gypsies coming.

It was the sixth of December, time of the new moon of the Cold Moon of 1901, and a hard cold had set upon northeastern North Carolina. The Committee brought Madam Snell Newman to the Cropsey house itself.

They led her into the dining room where Nell had last been seen, and there she startled her audience. She looked about the room, took a seat in the rocker beside the stove and rested her chin in both her hands.

—This is how and where Wilcox sat before he left the room with Ella Cropsey, who was sitting here beside him, she said.

Ollie Cropsey, who had been there, nodded it was so. Strong men felt ill at ease and in touch somehow with the supernatural. It was weird and marvelous and uncanny.

—Then Ella got up and sat near the stove, Madam Newman said.

Again Ollie nodded. God, she was acting out those last moments, before Nell went outside with Wilcox, before—

Madam Newman went to the hall–dining room door and put a hand to the knob, checked her watch, and then placed a hand on Ollie Cropsey's shoulder, as if she were Nell.

—Don't go away to New York, Madam Newman said to Ollie. Come out on the porch and we'll talk it over.

Hadn't it been thataway that night, over two weeks ago? Hadn't it? His checking his watch and calling her out like that? And poor Ollie, that gypsy making her play her sister and acting it out like that. How can that woman *know* all this?

Madam Newman left the room with Ollie and talked with her on the front porch for a while. Then she walked down to the front gate alone. She seemed in a trance and none dared follow her off the porch. Directly she turned and spoke to them.

—I heard a long, low whistle, through clairvoyance of course, and then I saw the Dayton wagon standing near the gate and beside it a man, closely muffled. He was of spare build and his features were not distinct. He and Wilcox seized Miss Cropsey, wrapped her closely around the neck and head with a robe, put her in the wagon and drove off.

The Committee of Five had done the right thing, people nodded at each other. They had thought it was a bad idea at first, but this gypsy was onto something. Why, Harry Greenleaf, when he starts something, he flies at it and covers everything. Who'd of ever thought a *gypsy* would be down here looking for Nell Cropsey?

Madam Newman and several Committee members clambered into a wagon and set out to retrace the route that had come to her in the trance, the route Wilcox and his accomplice had taken when they carried Nell Cropsey, chloroformed and wrapped in a robe or blanket one, to her death in an old well.

A small crew of curiosity seekers and reporters followed along on horseback and in other wagons, and this strange procession moved into the Pasquotank country beneath the dull metal-gray sky. It became an all-day December outing. No one had dressed warmly enough for such an expedition. Madam Newman insisted they go down one county trail after another, down the shell-pikes, miles and miles and all day in those wagons in the cold. No one had dressed for it.

Oh, they found two old wells, but neither yielded the body of Nell Cropsey. Madam Newman insisted they go on.

Wilcox was jealous, she told the Committee men. Nell was going off to New York, but he wanted to marry her and he feared he'd lose all chance if she went away. If he couldn't have her, no one would. So he carried her off and killed her and threw her down a deep old well. Madam Newman captivated them and led them through the country and the cold.

After twenty-five miles, they gave up.

—I can plainly see the place where the body is at the bottom of a well near an old house, but my power will not allow me to accurately judge the distance, she said. If anyone had a thought that Madam Newman was a sham, it went unvoiced. All were caught up in the excitement of the hunt, and they were willing to try anything.

Two of the Committee members had been elsewhere that day investigating the discovery of a body. When they got back to town, the report of yet another body found not ten miles from Elizabeth City had come in. Something would give sooner or later.

There were more old wells than two in the area. The Committee could leave nothing to chance, so its chairman, Harry Greenleaf, declared that the well search would go on.

The Diver

During that first week of December 1901, the Committee brought in a diver and engaged him indefinitely. He was John Edwards, an expert from the M. T. Cashin Submarine Contracting Company out of Norfolk. He would feel over the Pasquotank riverbed foot by foot, and if Nell Cropsey were there, he would find her.

Most had never seen a diver, so they swarmed by the river again to watch, though all they could see was the clockwork motion of the men manning the air pump on the pier, and then the air bubbles from Edwards's breathing as they broke the water's surface.

All the while there were mutterings against Jim Wilcox.

Day and night the diver crawled along the river bottom, and the ghastly signal of his success would be his hand's first touch on the beautiful girl, wherever her body lay in this black murky juniper river.

By the morning of December 5th, he had covered some twenty thousand square feet, beginning at the pier down which Hurricane Branch's bloodhounds had tracked. On December 6th, the search moved up to the marine railways, still to no avail. There was more muttering against Wilcox as the air-pump men worked in rhythm and the crowds watched the bubbles break the river surface beneath the cold platinum sky.

—The Cropsey family isn't taking as much interest in the diver as the general public, one of the Committee members remarked.

The case now involved rewards and a committee and a massive effort that overrode the tragedy of one family. It had become a cause, a crusade, and now it belonged to the town.

W. O. Saunders

Elizabeth City has been good to me.

I ran my paper, *The Independent*, here for pushing three decades, and folks the world over have paid attention.

People called me a crank, so I wrote myself up as such in *Collier's*.

Mordecai Ham, the revival preacher, came to Pasquotank and I exposed him, ran that anti-Semite out of town.

When I advocated pajamas as summer street dress, people laughed. I went to New York City and put on my silk pajamas and walked down Fifth Avenue and my picture ran in papers all over America.

But all this was way after the mystery of Beautiful Nell Cropsey put Elizabeth City on the map. Betsy Town, I like to call it.

Now the Cropsey case, the Wilcox trial—this was my first job.

I grew up over in Hertford, just west of Elizabeth City. I was the butcher's boy, and people said I was too smart for my own good. When I was ten or eleven, I decided I wanted to be either a Baptist preacher or a patent medicine faker—these were the two men who seemed to get to the most people.

Then I discovered Elbert Hubbard's editorials in one of the New York papers, and I realized that while the preacher and the faker were limited to the range of their own voices, Hubbard could be read throughout the world.

I decided to become an editor.

All of seventeen, I left home and went off to Norfolk up beyond the Great Dismal Swamp, landed a job on a paper there. But it was only work in the circulation department. Since I wanted to be an editor, I lost my enthusiasm and my new job and went back to my father's Hertford grocery and butcher shop.

And that was about the time Nell Cropsey vanished.

I read up on it, followed the case like a hawk on prey. I watched what happened to the people of Elizabeth City in the course of the long, drawn-out search for the girl. I kept files on it because I was fascinated, and I thought it might be worth something someday.

Now, in the late thirties, I realize I have probably been more engrossed in the Cropsey mystery than anything else that's come my way, other than trying to keep my paper afloat. But *The Independent* shut down in 1937 after twenty-nine years' publishing, and when I look through my files, the one I most often pull out and sift through is this one, the Cropsey case.

I was all set to put together a book with Jim Wilcox once. He agreed to tell his story, and I got a boat so we could go up the river where no one could possibly overhear our conversations. We were going to meet down at the R. C. Abbot wharf one Sunday morning in June 1932. I waited for hours.

Jim Wilcox never showed.

Now he's dead, Governor Bickett who pardoned him is dead, Roy Crawford shot himself, Nell's brother Will poisoned himself, and I seem to have only my files to piece together the story of what really occurred that night in 1901.

Soon after Nell Cropsey disappeared, Chief Dawson began to receive reports of sightings from various places around eastern North Carolina.

She was seen driving in a carriage with a man in South Mills, up the Pasquotank River near the Virginia line, on the second of December 1901.

W. O. Saunders

She was seen at Mackey's Ferry on the south shore of the Albemarle Sound, and then at Plymouth, only six miles from Mackey's, just a few days later.

One of my favorites was the report of a young woman supposed to be Nell Cropsey who was held for identification in Wilson, a tobacco market town over a hundred miles west of Elizabeth City, on the fourth of December. She and a male companion had spent the night of the third at Mrs. Ward's boarding house there, and the young woman paid the bills as the man seemed short of cash. He also got drunk and crashed around the house. Mrs. Ward reported them for disorderly conduct, but when the police arrived, the couple had slipped out. It wasn't until Turkey Creek that the reward-seeking officers Felton and Bryan overtook and arrested them at the Nichols house, fifteen miles out of Wilson.

Mayor Herring wired the Cropsey family and Chief Dawson, who sent back a detailed description of Nell Cropsey.

—Not a chance, said the Chief. I think it's the same girl they saw in Goose Nest and other places about there.

While he awaited Chief Dawson's return wire, Mayor Herring questioned the couple in Wilson. I suppose he thought he had her and was already seeing headlines and counting cash. He brought in a former schoolmate of Nell's to see if she could identify the girl one way or the other. And this schoolmate, a Miss Dyer, finally made a positive identification. It took her a while, apparently. She hesitated, saying it had been four years since she'd seen Nell and now Nell's hair was a good deal shorter than it had been.

So Nell Cropsey was found. Mayor Herring gleefully questioned the couple, who of course denied ever hearing of Nell Cropsey or Jim Wilcox either one.

—My name's MacKay Durham, the man said. Born in Durham County six miles from Durham town. I ain't lived there in fourteen years. Raleigh's my home.

But he couldn't seem to call up a street address for Mayor Herring, nor could he remember the name of the cotton mill where he said he'd been working.

—Not just now, anyways, Durham said.

Mayor Herring turned to the girl.

—My name is Miss Kersey. I was raised on a truck farm in Chattanooga. My mother's remarried, Mrs. Elizabeth Clark, and she lives there. I don't know any Jim Wilcox.

She was scared and confused and all of seventeen. She couldn't recall the place names of anywhere she had been recently. Miss Kersey told the mayor of Wilson, North Carolina, that MacKay Durham was a doctor who had brought her to eastern Carolina for some bear shooting, but that he was habitually intoxicated and had tried to kill her.

—Well, she said, maybe I *heard* of Wilcox.

I read these stories and jealously wished that I had been out there rambling about and filing amazing and bizarre reports for some paper, *any* paper. I read that the Associated Press searched the entire Chattanooga area and found that no one named Kersey or Clark had ever been heard of out there. I read how Mayor Herring got Chief Dawson's description and looked at the girl's teeth.

According to the description, Miss Cropsey had two teeth missing from her lower jaw, but the girl captured at Turkey Creek had one tooth missing from each side of her upper jaw. And the location of gold fillings was all different.

So they let Miss Kersey and her mad, drunk, bear-hunting, mill-working doctor go, and time and the world have swallowed them whole.

Chief Dawson was right, I thought. It was obviously the same couple that his authorized detective had been trailing through eastern Carolina and had even examined at the village of Speed several days earlier.

There was another intriguing piece about an elderly man traveling with a young lady in Philadelphia. Someone wired Chief Dawson that Nell Cropsey was found in the City of Brotherly Love, but when Dawson followed the lead, he discovered that the pair was registered at the Walton Hotel as *J. B. Murdock and niece, of New York City*.

Good Lord, I thought, how many there must be. Young girls traveling with men of all ages, the whole spectrum of assignations and elopements and tourist homes and cheap hotels everywhere from Speed, North Carolina, to Philadelphia, Pennsylvania. Chief Dawson was going to have to track down every lead or see that someone else did—kicking in doors and frightening anxious, mismatched couples and demanding their identities. Someone was going to have to get a look at all these girls and know for certain that the latest Nell Cropsey was not really her but, instead, some other terrified stray. Lord, I thought, I don't know how Dawson's going to do it.

But it was all very exciting and tragic and full of the promise of adventure for me, a seventeen-year-old butcher's boy working in his dad's miserable meat shop in Hertford, reading up on the big mystery in the town next door, daydreaming about being an editor. I had no way of knowing the day would come and not only would I be one, but H. L. Mencken himself, the master of American letters, would put in print the greatest compliment I've ever received. Ed Aydlett, the political boss of Elizabeth City, tried to shut me and *The Independent* down, churchmen fired gunshots into my house, and I was hauled through the county courts time and again when my editorial candor was mistaken for libel. But the ordeals were well worth it when this notice came to my attention:

—If the South had forty editors like W. O. Saunders, wrote Mencken, its problems would disappear within five years.

OLLIE CROPSEY

Nell had been gone two-and-a-half weeks when we heard the loathsome stories from Norfolk.

A young man named Edward Kelly, a patent solicitor, came to Seven Pines in December 1901 and told us the most treacherous and base tale. He said that he had met Nell on the Seaboard Air Line train into Norfolk on the morning of November 22d, a day and a half after she was first missed. She was supposedly traveling under the name of Jessie Baker, who was a girlfriend of ours from Elizabeth City.

This Kelly said he talked with her on the train, spent the day with her, dined with her, and saw her off on the Old Dominion steamer that night, alone and with no baggage. She was wearing new shoes, a light jacket, and a red waist with brass buttons, he said, and he alerted the police chief of Norfolk and the newspapers.

He also said this girl was missing two teeth.

How could Nell have bought new shoes or a jacket or changed her buttons? I wondered. And I know for certain she had only a nickel in her pocket when she stepped into the hall with Jim Wilcox.

Kelly said the girl had mentioned that she would be visiting Baltimore for six to eight weeks.

Who did Nellie know in *Baltimore*? I couldn't believe him, and he so infuriated Papa that there was a nasty scene and almost a fight. Papa had already been enraged over the incident of the spiritualist, Madam Newman. He'd sworn that anyone else who came to our house with incantations or hocus-pocus or any other unholy mess would get out quicker than they got in. And he meant it.

—You're a fake! he shouted at Kelly and flew at him in a rage. There would have been a fight but the policeman who had come with Kelly kept them apart. Papa made them leave, and we were more upset than ever.

There was even another version of this story of Kelly's, and it was far worse for us if such a thing were possible.

In the papers it was reported that Nell had a traveling companion named Guy Hall and that Nell and this man spent the night of November 22d in a Main Street boarding house in Norfolk. Then she caught the next morning's boat for Washington, D.C. We all knew very well who Guy Hall was.

He was a good friend of Jim Wilcox.

Guy Hall, the papers said, had been turned out of the state of Virginia for his role in the Hall-Cannon affair. A man named Cannon had hired Guy Hall to seduce Mrs. Cannon or somehow ruin her character in order to win a divorce from her. It was a sordid business, and we had not known about it, though we knew of Guy Hall. He had come to Elizabeth City not too long before and become Jim's friend. Guy Hall was a gymnast, a trickster, and Lord knows what else.

Imagine Nell spending the night with such a creature.

They were all vicious stories, and with each one came

reporters seeking our comments and thoughts. We Cropseys were a big, loving family. We had never been invaded and hurt by the world at large. I lost so much privacy and dignity from the way I felt we were treated then that I have never sought society in the long years since. We were curiosities, objects of pity, and the whole history of our lives since then has been isolated and abnormal for that reason.

Mama, in her grief, would interrupt her vigil in the cupola and come down and talk with the reporters. She thought somehow it might do some good, her words might reach Nell—and she needed to defend her own.

—I didn't favor Jim much, she said, but the girls had a good time with him, so I didn't object to his coming. But he was changeable. Sometimes he would barely speak to me for three or four days and then he would come back and bring flowers. Nell wasn't in the habit of meeting young men. If she had been I shouldn't have been so uneasy that night and would not have given the alarm. I hardly know whether or not to think this Norfolk girl is Nell—there have been so many rumors and I am so much troubled.

I feared Mama would break under the strain.

When the *New York Journal* and the Associated Press both announced that the search for my sister in Baltimore was being limited to *certain Baltimore institutions*, Papa said he would sue.

How could they print such vile things?

I was heartbroken for Nell and for us all.

Eventually word came that the girl had been found. She was a look-alike for Nell but not Nell at all. She was Sara Baker, a pretty milliner from Franklin, Virginia. I was relieved, of course, but terribly disappointed, too, because it meant that perhaps Nellie was in the river after all. The dragging and cannon firing was still going on.

Nell had been gone three weeks when Papa said it would be a relief if her dead body were to be found. I wept and grieved and blamed myself.

TALK

They said Jim Wilcox was proud of his notoriety, that he hung around on street corners in town, smiling brazenly without a trace of worry.

They also said he ran away, disappeared himself because he was scared and guilty as hell. Though he had only gotten permission to go down and stay at his kinfolks' in south Pasquotank, he just looked bad no matter what.

On December 9th, 1901, there was another mass rally, and this time a thousand people came and the county courthouse overflowed. Harry Greenleaf, the vigilante chairman, read an open letter from William Cropsey to the town.

> The police officials and the Committee have done all human agency could do to restore my daughter, without success. I shall always believe that Jim Wilcox was instrumental in my daughter's disappearance and if she is dead I believe his hand or the hand of his hireling is responsible for her death. Sometime when this life shall cease and we shall stand before the presence of the great Judge I believe we shall learn how and when he murdered my daughter and that the justice he may escape will be dealt with then.

Harry Greenleaf went on with great drama.

—After chasing shadows and rainbows, at last we have a tangible clue, he declared.

A whiskey bottle had been found on the sand beach in front of the Cropsey house. One of the local saloon keepers told the Committee he'd sold one just like it to Jim Wilcox.

—Let's make the one who knows all about this affair disclose it, said Greenleaf.

They applauded wildly and came up with an additional two hundred dollars in donations for the Committee to fund its work. They despised Jim Wilcox with a collective passion and could have lynched him then and there. The blood of that town was boiling.

JIM WILCOX

Everywhere I went folks were asking me Jim where is that girl? Even my aunt down the county, but I told her and the rest of em, Ask the Committee, they know all about these things. I went down there for a while in December while they were searching. Daddy said people were a damn sight more interested in pinning something on me than they were in finding Nell. Get out of town, he told me. Lawyer Aydlett agreed and fixed it with the mayor so I could clear out while the heat was on. Everybody'll know where you are, he said.

When I came back into town there in the middle of the month, I happened to run into Guy Hall, the athlete from Virginia. We were at the railway depot and I got to sporting with his trained dog. All of a sudden I looked up and there's a crowd gathering and staring at me while I was making Guy's dog do tricks on the station platform. And before long there was newspapermen showing up and asking, always asking.

—Been away, haven't you, Jim?

I can hear em now.

—Been to see your gal?

—Where you keeping her, Jim?

—What've you done with Nell Cropsey?

I could of trounced somebody and beat the hell out of em, but it's always been like that since Nell disappeared.

—Hold your temper, Jim, Guy Hall said, they just trying to rile you, provoke you into something you'd be sure to regret.

—Ask the Committee, I said, they seem to know everything. Yes, it's true I gave her back her parasol and her photographs and we'd had a disagreement sometime before but that wouldn't cause her to take her life I don't think. People put up lies about me. You can hear a lot about me if you listen to em.

The crowd there at the station kept staring in such a taunting way, and the newsmen kept badgering.

—When were you going to get married, Jim?

I can hear em now.

—Didn't you tell different ones that she would never go to New York?

Well, I never said that and Nell and I never talked once about getting married. But we wasn't engaged.

—Jim, you heard Cropsey's blaming you for the whole thing?

I answered I couldn't understand it. I'd always been friends of the whole family. I couldn't account for it, any of it.

Guy Hall collared his dog and we cleared out of the depot. That's telling em, Jim, he said as we were leaving. That's telling em good.

OLLIE CROPSEY

I was sick when they came in from the drag boats with a piece of dress goods. Oh, we tried to believe it couldn't be, but we knew then she was dead in that cold river. Till then we had held out hope that Nell might still be alive. Even those awful cruel rumors from Norfolk weren't this bad. That sealed it, and after that we never expected to see her alive again.

Mama kept up her vigil in the tower till she was nearly crazy with fatigue and grief. We tried to keep our feelings from the little children, but they knew. The detective Uncle Andrew sent down to us, Connor, stayed with us till he simply threw up his hands and gave up and said in all his forty years he had never run up against a case so intricate and hopeless. We knew she was in that river. About the time Mister Connor left to go back north, Uncle Andrew sent a submarine lighting device to us to help the diver as he searched the dark river bottom for poor Nell. It was the week before Christmas, and by then she'd been gone a month. I didn't mind at all when we moved away from Seven Pines not long after that. I began to use the side door because if I went out the front there was that cold black river.

How it haunted me and haunts me still.

W. O. SAUNDERS

The longer Nell Cropsey was missing, the more fascinated I became with the case and with reading whatever news stories we could get about it over there in Hertford.

There were two divergent reports from men who had been out in boats on the Pasquotank at exactly the time Miss Cropsey had stepped out to say good-night or good-bye or whatever it was she said to Jim Wilcox. One report had it that a tugboat towing a barge pulled out of the Knobbs Creek shingle mill and headed downriver at exactly eleven P.M. The tug captain said his boat came abreast of the pier near the Cropsey home about fifteen minutes later and that when it did, a white sixteen-foot skiff appeared in the moonlight. That would have been ten minutes from the time Nell and Jim went into the front hall, according to both Jim and Miss Olive Cropsey.

The tug captain said the skiff pulled out of the shadows of the wharf and headed westward, upriver, toward the town a quarter-mile away. He saw one man seated in the stern and a second man rowing, and that was all.

The second report came from New Bern. A local man said he'd talked with the officer of a revenue cutter there some days after Nell Cropsey vanished. The officer said that his boat had been anchored in the Pasquotank out from that same pier on the night she disappeared, and that his watch declared that nothing unusual occurred. Had anyone plunged from the pier into the river or taken a boat from there, his watch would most assuredly have noticed, the officer said.

But Len Owens and a mate on the *Ray*, a launch plying upriver and passing the Cropsey house at 11:15 that night, seemed to corroborate the tug captain's story. I heard and read that they saw a skiff glide across the river from the opposite shore to the Cropsey side and then skim under the bushes near the summerhouse.

I've mulled over these stories for years. None of them ever showed up as evidence in any testimony, yet Jim Wilcox might easily have been lynched with a rumor like the white skiff story floating around.

On the other hand, terror is a whimsical beast. Between wild rumor and vigilante fever, the town was crazed. And if the same beast that destroyed Robespierre could claim Jim Wilcox, it could turn and destroy virtually anyone.

Even the father of the missing girl was not immune.

A letter from George Hotteso of Rocky Mount, North Carolina, arrived for William Cropsey on December 21st, 1901. Hotteso supposedly wrote that a young man had left Nell Cropsey in that town with a half-breed woman named Mary Kenny, and that Nell wouldn't give her name. She was afraid of her father, afraid he would kill her and the young man both.

Two members of the Committee went to investigate, and two days before Christmas, three disparate stories came back from Rocky Mount.

One said Miss Cropsey had been identified and was being taken back to Elizabeth City by the Committee men.

Another said she had disappeared from Mary Kenny's house and had given the Committee the slip.

The third report said that the Hotteso letter had been forged by none other than William Cropsey. And, further, the Committee claimed to have caught Cropsey in several falsehoods, confronted him, and found his manner indifferent.

SUSPICIOUS FINGER POINTING AT CROPSEY!
DID HE HIDE THE GIRL?

I clipped that story from the front page of the Raleigh *News and Observer*, and I would look at it from time to time over the years and wonder, especially in light of some of the dark and horrifying tales I've heard people in Elizabeth City tell about William Cropsey and what really became of his daughter, Beautiful Nell.

CHRISTMASTIDE

The wind had blown dark clouds across the waxing moon, and men in boats on the river saw, or thought they saw, a ghost skiff as the shadows from the moonlight shifted.

After a month, the search for Nell Cropsey became an endless sifting of sand. The river dragging was abandoned, the diver was sent home, the reports and letters from hither and yon proved false or inconclusive. So traceless was her disappearance that by Christmas 1901, the family and the town had given up hope—not of finding her alive, but of finding her at all.

THE TOWN

OLLIE CROPSEY

I didn't know what to think, whether to laugh or cry when Papa told us he was going to move us to Elizabeth City.

He had read an advertisement that John Fearing had placed in one of the New York papers wanting someone to farm land near his place on the Pasquotank River in eastern North Carolina. Papa loved farming, and he thought in the South we could have crops and some sort of garden almost year round.

So he accepted the offer, and Uncle Andrew paid first rent on the land.

John Fearing sent Papa back a delighted reply and a bundle of commerce pamphlets that he read over and over and showed the rest of us. The pamphlets said the Pasquotank was a cornucopia offering a brilliant harvest from its lands and waters. They said the Pasquotank was very much like the south of France in the demeanor of its climate.

The south of France!

Papa made a trip down first, and then we all came in April of 1898, and we stayed at the Fearing home because our furniture had been misdirected and shipped to New Jersey and we hadn't found a house yet anyway.

The very first things we saw in Elizabeth City were crates and crates of strawberries and the herring criers in the streets. I heard one old man say at market that he'd follow strawberries all over the world, he loved them so.

We had seen a picture in one of Mister Fearing's pamphlets of the strawberry pickers who camped beside the fields at harvest. They wore bandanas and scarves and wide-brimmed straw hats and carried shallow trays into the fields by day. They brought the berries into the grading shed, where they were sorted and packed and put on a one-mule, two-wheel wagon headed for market. Except for the wagon driver and one grader and the bald overseer, all the rest were black people.

They must have broken their backs picking berries for that old man.

Anyway, this is the sort of thing Papa showed us and talked about before he brought us to the South. Our whole family, other than Uncle Andrew, was against our move and I was too. I was young then and all my friends and cousins lived in New York.

We were the Cropseys of Brooklyn. We were among the Old Dutch that built Brooklyn, and New York too. Our ancestor Casparse came from Germany or Holland to New Amsterdam. Then the Dutch spread out into Jersey and Long Island, and Papa says they called it Brukelen then. Our name changed to Crasparse, then Craspar, Cropsow, Cropsie, Cropsy, then finally Cropsey like it is now. I've even gotten mail from a woman who spelled it Crapsey who must be some sort of cousin. She sent me a poem about Nell.

Cropsey Avenue is a big street in Brooklyn, named after our relative James Cropsey, who led the Kings County Buckskins against the British in 1812. He was a hero. When he got the contract to build Fort Hamilton at the Verrazano Narrows, he walked the highway between his home and the fort site so much that they named it for him. Cropsey Avenue. He was called Boss Cropsey because he was a builder, and he built good solid forts. He built Fort Wadsworth, Fort Totten, Fort Schuyler, and he died while he had Fortress Monroe under construction at Hampton Roads just as the Civil War started. He was our kin.

We belonged to the New Utrecht Reform Church, which Boss Cropsey had rebuilt using stones from the original Dutch church there. He had the pews nailed down so tightly and solidly that when it was remodeled way later they marveled at his diligence and said Boss Cropsey had built the church just like one of his forts.

This was our stock.

We buried our little infant brother in the graveyard of the New Utrecht church, long before Papa brought us to Elizabeth City. He gave up the position of excise commissioner of New Utrecht to go south. We were good Tammany Democrats, and we left it all behind.

If an uneducated black man can do THIS . . . was the caption beneath another of the pamphlet photographs. It was of a black man in dark baggy pants and a collarless white cotton shirt with thick suspenders and sleeves rolled. He was holding a hoe and standing in front of fifty bushels or more of peas they said he brought in from one unfertilized acre.

Is it any wonder Papa wanted to drop everything and move here to farm? Just scratch the earth, they said, and crops would come in almost by themselves. Potatoes could be in the ground by late February so Papa said there could be three crops a year on the same land. He was going to grow potatoes, he said, and have a big garden. We've always had big, beautiful gardens, over at Seven Pines and then around the point at the house we lost when Uncle Andrew died, and out here on Southern Avenue too. I remember Papa calling us out to the porch at Seven Pines when he brought in the ripe, round tomatoes. He would polish them with his handkerchief and hand them to us saying, here's one for my lovely daughter and here's one for my lovely daughter, and so on till each daughter had a tomato and we'd thank him and laugh.

When our furniture finally did arrive, we had to saw off the tops of the posts of our lovely four-poster beds so they'd fit in the house. It was spring and everything was so lush here, and Elizabeth City was so busy then.

FIRE AND ICE

William Cropsey, new to town, picked up the local papers and saw columns after column of ads seeking game, waterfowl, fish, and terrapin for the great markets of the northern cities.

Great seines in the Albemarle stretched four miles end to end when let out fully, and the herring came in at fifty to a hundred thousand in a single haul. Where once it had taken boats with sixteen or more oarsmen to shoot the nets, now, with steam engines, five hauls could be made in the time it had taken to draw three.

And now, with refrigeration, ice-making by condensers, and tubes and steam compressors unknown to the world before the 1870s, and the railroad with all its sidewheel steamboat connections, the Albemarle's lands and waters could be opened up like never before. Out of Elizabeth City came Doctor Palemon John's Republican weekly, the *North Carolinian*, ceaselessly trumpeting to the world the resources and possibilities in a land devoid of industry and money, its people broken and broke from their War of romantic and delusive conception and its ruinous, fatal conclusion.

Steam, ice, and the railroad made it all possible.

Fish, produce, and game could be in New York within twenty hours of a day's picking or shooting or seine hauling. Shad, rockfish, mullet, blues, Spanish mackerel, chub, perch, sturgeon, menhaden, trout, spot, hogfish, croaker, flounder—they were packed on ice and shipped fresh. Twenty thousand acres in the Albemarle and Pamlico Sounds yielded oysters, hard- and soft-shell crabs, prawn, and shrimp.

Professional gunners called market hunters brought their kill into Elizabeth City from Currituck, fowl they had bagged from blinds in the shallows of the sound, from sink boxes in the shoals, the reward for waiting and freezing and sipping whiskey in the cold wet fall and winter dark before dawn. They broke the mornings' silence with their muzzle loaders and their double-barrel breech loaders and their punt guns, homemade cannons with barrels up to ten feet long and two-inch bores that, filled with chopped nails, did not give the birds a second chance. The market hunters brought their kill in and the

The Narrows: Pasquotank River at Elizabeth City, about 1905

birds were stuffed in barrels around ice-filled stove-pipes and shipped away to Baltimore and Philadelphia and New York City, where drummers banged tavern tables and called for meals of feathers and oysters.

This tideland, this coastal plain, was a cornucopia inexhaustible, the commercial circulars said, and steam, ice, and the railroad made it fully exploitable. By the turn of the century, Elizabeth City was booming.

And William Cropsey was new to town and glad to be, glad to have brought his big family down to Pasquotank and into the heart of the horn of plenty.

JIM WILCOX

I liked em all, but it was Nell I liked from the first.

She had older sisters more my age. There was Louise and Alletta, but they were both big, broad women, and there was Ollie. Now Ollie was a good-looking girl, but she was tall and towered over me. I've heard she's right much of a looker yet, but I ain't seen her. All I asked since I come back from prison was just a little time with her to talk about it and get it straight. Just ten minutes.

Nell was sixteen and pretty and about my height. I was twenty-one at the time and my daddy was high sheriff of all Pasquotank County.

I just had two sisters, Sadie and Annie Mae, but the Cropseys had a big family. I never paid much attention to the younger ones, except maybe Will Cropsey. He was younger than Nell, and we went duck hunting or boating together once, I can't recall. Now Will, he knew a lot more about this thing than he let on. He could of cleared it up. He was staying up in Norfolk when Mama was getting up the petitions to the governor for me to be pardoned. They told me that when Will Cropsey heard I might be getting out, he poisoned himself to death.

Up at the old Monticello Hotel on Granby Street in Norfolk they told me, the one burned down New Year's Eve 1919, and the water from the firehoses run down the side and froze and that old hotel looked like a ice castle. That's where he done it.

I got introduced to Nell one evening in June '98, and I come calling on her one afternoon two weeks later. Sent a boy around with a card inviting her out buggy riding with me and she said yes. I could rent Beam S., the thoroughbred stallion, out of Fletcher's stable and a carriage, that's what. I'd come on Sundays and Tuesdays and Thursdays, then, after a while, I come by every afternoon. By then I guess I'd asked Nell to be my girl and she said yes she would.

We went to whatever shows come through town. Up to the Academy of Music. *The Real Widow Brown*, that was one. *Jolly Night*, there were always shows trouping through. I took her to all of em.

We'd go out sailing, too, when there was enough of a breeze. We only went by ourselves twice and we stayed out way late, ten or eleven at night both times, and when I brought her in I caught hell from her old man, all six foot six of him. I wish old man Cropsey had come out and told all *he* knew. I told Johnny Tuttle I'd like to get the old man out in a boat and tell him if he didn't explain to me what happened with Nell that night I'd put a blowtorch to his feet. That's what I said, but I knew I'd never do anything like that, never get away with it if I did. He wouldn't talk anyway.

We'd go swimming there at the sandy beach once they'd moved to their own place. That was the old Preyer house with the tower, but the Cropseys called it Seven

Pines. Water was real shallow straight out, and you could go out toward the river channel thirty yards or more and it'd only be four foot deep. Old man Cropsey anchored a raft out where it was deep enough to dive off.

There was baseball at Waters Park just around the bend, downriver a bit from the Cropseys. I played infield and Roy Crawford who used to call on Ollie did too. He was there that night Nell disappeared. Went crazy years later after I was off in prison and shot himself dead. I didn't like him much, but he was a crackerjack first baseman. Our ball club played teams got up in other towns, like the Kitty Hawk club from down the Banks. They give us a good run once.

That summer of '98 when I got to be good friends with Nell and all the Cropseys, they had moonlight cruises on the steamers with singing and dancing and the town cornet band playing. My aunt died along about then, the one that was married to my uncle James that I was named for. He was a deputy sheriff, but that fall they voted Daddy out and the Democrats were in. Didn't bother the Cropseys none—they were Democrats up north from way back.

NEWBEGUN

Newbegun was near Weeksville in south Pasquotank County, and the township pollkeeper John Brothers lived there.

One Monday in October of 1894, Deputy James Wilcox came to Brothers's house wanting a look at the voting rolls, but Brothers argued with him and told him to get out of the house and that he didn't have to show any Republican deputy the voting rolls.

James Wilcox stood his ground, so Brothers got a

cudgel out of a closet and came at Wilcox with the big stick raised. He backed Wilcox out onto the porch, where Wilcox drew a pistol and shot as Brothers struck him head and body with the cudgel. Brothers got hit in the arm and stomach, and before he died the next day, he swore that Wilcox had been standing when he fired the pistol.

Wilcox swore it was self-defense and said he had fired only when Brothers attacked him and knocked him down. Ginnie Perkins, who was in the kitchen, said she heard a couple of blows from a stick, then the pistol shots, and then she heard Brothers's mother saying that if her son had minded her, this wouldn't have happened.

Three justices of the peace, including Teddy Wilson and Harry Greenleaf, held a preliminary hearing four days after the shooting and bound James Wilcox over to superior court, where he was tried for murder in March 1895. Lawyer Ed Aydlett defended him, put him on the stand in his own defense. Then they put a doctor up to testify who told the court that the wound in John Brothers's arm could only have been made if Brothers had his arm raised.

The jury went out fourteen hours and came back with a verdict that James Wilcox was guilty of murder in the second degree. The judge sentenced him to fifteen years in prison, but Lawyer Aydlett appealed to the state supreme court. A dozen men went Wilcox's ten thousand dollar bond, among them Doctor John, the Republican editor, and Cale Parker, a farmer friend of the Wilcox family.

A year later James Wilcox was acquitted. Six months after that he was hauled in on and pled guilty to a charge of assault and battery. Six weeks later, he pled guilty to carrying a concealed weapon.

This was the man for whom Jim Wilcox, Nell Cropsey's new beau, was named. People talked about bad blood in a family, and how it could flow quietly for years and then suddenly just flare up, crazy like. When Jim went down to south Pasquotank for his aunt's funeral in '98, the Cropseys couldn't help but hear the talk.

OLLIE CROPSEY

The first Christmas we were down south, Jim gave Nell a dish with a silver frame and handle. The second Christmas he gave her a gold pin with a red jewel of some sort set in it. She'd show me the photographs they exchanged every so often, just cheap little five-and-dime-store pictures.

Our family stayed down on the Outer Banks in the summer of 1900, and Jim made regular Sunday trips to Nags Head to see Nellie. One Sunday she came in after a walk with him and said she had something to show me.

It was a ring he had just given her, with her initials *E.M.C.* on the inside.

TRUCK FARMER

William Cropsey marveled.

Farmers were studying chemistry just as Jefferson and Ruffin, who fired the first shot at Sumter, had urged them to do long ago. They were improving their tools, draining and fencing their flat boggy lands. They used manures and fertilizers, rotated their crops, and they tried a diversity of crops theretofore unheard of.

Truck farming, it was called.

Pasquotank was growing crops that could be picked, cut, graded, boxed, barreled, and then shipped right out from the field: tomatoes, cabbages, blackberries, Big Blues from the huckleberry savannahs, Chickasaw and wild goose plums, dewberries, peaches, cantaloupes, and muskmelons. And in one pamphlet was a picture of a three-year-old pear tree bearing fifty-nine fully matured pears!

There was something called the *soja* bean, though local farmers quickly disregarded the second syllable. Bayside Plantation, downriver from where the Cropseys settled, was the first place in the United States to grow soybeans, which were found to be an economical horse and cattle feed.

Just scratch the earth . . .

Cropsey marveled, and the produce kept coming in. Irish potatoes in the summer and fall, peanuts standing in brown harvest shocks to dry, midwinter cukes for extravagant northern tables, six cuttings of alfalfa a season, Norton and mouseleaf yams, horsetooth corn.

Years later people would see the old man William Cropsey selling vegetables door to door from a basket he carried slung around his arm.

—Do you recall the mystery of Beautiful Nell Cropsey who vanished one night and Jim Wilcox her beau who suffered for it? Yes? Well, that vendor is her father.

But that was much, much later.

When William Cropsey answered John Fearing's ad in 1898 and rented sixty-five acres from Fearing between the black river and the fairground racetrack and moved his huge family south that April, he became the largest truck farmer in the Albemarle section, with expectations of a June 1899 Irish potato crop of ten thousand barrels.

JIM WILCOX

I always heard a trip to Nags Head was worth ten days in the best hospital in the land. The Cropseys must of heard it, too, they were staying down there during the summer of 1900.

I'd catch the steamer *Neuse*, dark old thing, Saturday evenings when it pulled out for Manteo after the southbound came in from Norfolk. Never had to wait much, it was pretty fair about being on time, except for that time the cyclone stranded the boat up on Paupers Point for half a year. On the way down to Manteo Captain Davis'd get all sweated up telling about it.

At Manteo, there'd be Captain Daniels smoking a pipe and sitting under a fig tree like he won't expecting anything even though we come in every Saturday night right at that time. Me and whoever else was going over would hire him to take us to the soundside landing at Nags Head. He'd make twenty knots I bet in his sailboat.

It'd be eleven or so when he'd leave us there where the shanties and shacks and pier was falling in and we'd go on over to the hotel and wake the night clerk and get stowed away.

This one time, it was July 17th, 1900, I'll never forget, Sunday morning after breakfast and Nellie and I went out walking on the wide hotel porches where it smelled all mixed of salt spray and kitchen and somebody's morning cigar. I pulled a little package, all wrapped up, out of my pocket and give it to her.

—It's your birthday, Nell, I said. It was a ring I got at Hathaway's and had em put her initials on the inside.

—Why, Jim, ain't you something? she said, and she gave me a little hug when she opened it and saw what it was.

HURRICANE SEASON

It was hurricane season, September 1900, late that summer after Jim Wilcox had given his girl a ring, when a bicycle mechanic named Wilbur Wright from Dayton, Ohio, showed up in Elizabeth City asking directions to the Outer Banks village of Kitty Hawk. Storm winds were raging as the autumnal equinox approached, flooding the low country, and in town the creeks had risen enough to overflow yards and streets and thin, drooping willow branches were everywhere dragging in the water.

Wright hired Israel Perry and his schooner *Curlicue*, and they made their way slowly through two days of awful weather, the cordage and spars creaking all the way and both foresail and mainsail ripped loose by the storm. Wright wouldn't eat Perry's foul-smelling food— he was half starved and drowned when he finally got to Kitty Hawk. People said it was crazy as hell to go down there during hurricane season doing what he was doing, working on gliders till late October. But he came back again for six weeks in '01, for two months in '02, and for three months in '03 when, a week and a day before Christmas, this man Wright and his brother Orville brought a glider with a motor strapped to it out of their hangar at Kitty Hawk and flew the world's first aeroplane.

Back in hurricane season, 1901, the news came that a crazy man named Czolgosz had gunned down the president up in Buffalo, New York. And it was about that time when Nell Cropsey and Jim Wilcox started to go sour on each other.

OLLIE CROPSEY

Along about in September that year, I heard them arguing.

—If you're going to act like this, then you'd best stay home the rest of the season, I heard Nell tell Jim. But he kept coming and calling on her. Then Uncle Andrew brought our cousin Carrie and left her for a visit with us. She had been down the year before, so she already knew Jim. With Nell and Jim a bit shaky, he paid Carrie almost as much attention as he was paying Nellie those days.

Once in the kitchen we were talking about how queer Jim could be, and Mama told Uncle Andrew she was becoming fearful of him and that she had forebodings that he would harm Nell someday. Imagine, *forebodings*!

And Nell said, Uncle Andrew, I've made up my mind not to have anything to do with Jim. Sometimes he's very nice, but then he's eccentric and has such a peculiar way.

With Carrie there, Nell and Jim seemed to get on a little better, and they went around all three of them together. Sometimes I'd make it four. It was lovely then, that warm lapse after the harvest, when the cypress trees along the river turned a rusty gold.

THE SOULWINNER

In early October 1901, the churches in Elizabeth City pooled their money and brought one of America's most famous evangelists to town for a ten-day revival.

His name was George Rutledge Stuart, and good God was he popular.

In Memphis, the building where he spoke was so

packed a man fell through a window where he had been watching from outside and was arrested, whereupon he begged to see Stuart.

—Is this the first man you ever arrested for breaking in to hear a preacher? Stuart asked.

—Yes, said the police.

—Well, turn him loose for good luck.

In Dayton, it took the great dining hall of the Cash Register Factory to hold the eight thousand who came back for more after Stuart's regular lecture series had run its course. In Portsmouth, Ohio, the church was so jammed when he arrived that he had to be lifted and passed above the congregation by hand in order to reach the platform.

Stuart was tall, rawboned, blue-eyed, with a long nose and drooping ears and a mustache, his hair swept back to the left. He wore a dark suit, a white shirt and waistcoat, and a dark, thin bow tie. He chartered buggies, automobiles, whole trains: whatever it took to get him and his message to the people.

And everywhere he went he appeared as the Lord's man against drink. His enemies knew he was a zealot who would accept no less than total prohibition. They burned his barn and horses twice and warned him if he didn't let up they'd come after his wife and children with the torch.

Stuart rode the rails and ignored the threats.

He came into a North Carolina that had beaten prohibition three to one twenty years before. And he came into the town of Elizabeth City, with its thirteen saloons and plenty of working men starving for whiskey at the end of the day.

He joked and called himself one of the ugliest men in America. He made Elizabeth City laugh, and he drew increasing numbers to his evening sessions at the First Baptist Church. Stuart broke their hearts, telling how his father had been ruined by the Civil War and driven to drink, till he himself was converted at a Quaker camp meeting and begged his dissipated father to do the same. Then Stuart locked his own father inside a granary to pray and kept guard outside so his old man couldn't slip out to meet the Devil and a jug of forty-rod.

Stuart held a special session at the Academy of Music on Sunday, October 6th. He came loaded for bear and gave them both barrels in the theater built where Sam Williams used to run his saloon.

Stuart pointed to a boy in the first row.

—Come here, boy, up to the platform. And when the boy was on stage with Stuart and in full view of all, Stuart shouted,

—What is the raw material for the gin mill? Our American boys!

He put his arm around the boy's shoulder.

—And this great drunkard factory is ever crying, Bring on more boys!

An Irishwoman stood and cried, The saloons have got my boy, the saloons have got my darling boy!

He paused and asked, Please give me something to represent the saloon. Somebody brought Stuart the smoke-blackened chimney from an oil lamp.

—What shall I do with it? he asked Elizabeth City, shouting.

—Smash it! came the answer.

Stuart threw down the globe and trampled the glass till it was broken to shards, while the crowd stomped and cheered.

—Brother! he cried.

—Sister! he cried.

—My life work is to push the bottle from every drunk-ard's hand. Everyone in this great audience, men and women, who will join the fight to vote for closing the sa-loons, stand on your feet!

The crowd was up almost at once, and a voice from the stage said, Thank God and Stuart, everyone is up.

When the soulwinner wrapped up his ten-day session in October 1901, the town was in a white heat.

JIM WILCOX

Nell joined the Methodist church a few days after that preacher Stuart left. She wanted me to join, too. Wanted me not to drink anything anymore, and we argued bad. I weren't a drunkard, not then anyway. I didn't get to drinking till after I come back from the prison farm. Then I had me a little grocery out on Ehringhaus Street. Nobody, no trade come except just a few old boys, friends of mine. People were whispering behind my back everywhere I went. It was pretty damn bad the way this town felt to me then. People said that's Jim Wilcox's store—he carried off Nell Cropsey and come out of prison mean.

Just those old boys come by and we just sat around that store of mine and waited for trade, but we could of waited for the stars to drop. Most days one of them'd bring a bottle and we'd pass it around till it was done. Then somebody'd go fetch another one. It was prohibi-tion in the twenties but whiskey was easy to get in Eliz-abeth City. They made it down in the swamps, down at a still at East Lake so big they worked it in shifts and the boys went to work by a whistle. No tax man was ever gon take on them white liquor boys down in their own swamp.

Whiskey come into town by boat. Cars'd run it on up to Norfolk where the real traffic was, sailors and merchantmen. Here in town a fellow over by Tiber Creek kept liquor around. If you wanted some he'd reach down onto the creekwharf pilings at a certain spot and run his hand down in the water. He'd feel around for a nail underwater and then pull up a line that was tied to the nail. The whiskey bottles were tied onto the line every foot or so. He'd sell you a bottle and drop the line with the rest on it back into the creek. More come in regular so he never ran out, and nobody stole from him cause he carried a gun.

After the store went bust, George Madrin and I worked building cabinets and coffins and doing some upholstery in the shop back of Ziegler's Funeral Home on South Road Street. George and I were a right good team. We had a house together then, a shanty behind the city market, and we used to sit out on stumps in the yard and tell stories to boys that'd come by.

I got to where I never wanted to be out on the street anymore, so I made a path I could follow off the street, from my sister's to Johnny Tuttle's garage, through the arch at Ziegler's where the hearses go, then on to my shop out back and over to Zip Bailey's gas station. This path of mine ran the same direction as Church Street, but it was a cut-through so I didn't have to see nobody but who I wanted to.

We'd hang around and talk at Zip's. Next to his place was the Duke Inn where men'd bring their girlfriends and sometimes forget to pull down the shades. We'd sit there watching at Zip Bailey's and have us a real show. I guess I scared some of the boys from Zip's one night. I was riding in somebody's car and there was a pistol in the glove box that I pulled out. We saw some of the fellows walking west on Church Street. Pull over slow, I said to whoever was driving. The boys on the street could see I was twirling that gun and I asked em real slow and cool, How you boys doing tonight? They ran off double quick, never said a word. People were scared of me generally.

No, I never did give much thought to joining the Methodist church. I tried going once when I come back from prison and people wouldn't even sit in the same pew with me. If that's Christianity I didn't want none of it.

I wonder what Nell would of said about that.

THE CIRCUS

The canvas train had come into town before dawn, October 22d, 1901. The boss hostler got the tents over to the fairgrounds, half a mile behind Seven Pines, away from the river. They put the kingpole of the three-peak tent up by hand, and it was a pure-t sonofabitch to do it using only a double block and fall. After that, the other two peak poles could go up by horse power, for there was no shortage of three-quarter-ton Percherons that stood sixteen hands high on heavy caulked shoes.

The boss hostler cried out in the dawn:

—Haul and hurry—find that damned stake and chain wagon—kick the plankers—fit the bleachers together or there's no show today.

Matériel poured onto the lot—hay, straw, oats, bran, bales of shavings, cords of wood to keep a head of steam up on the calliope.

Later that morning, the second train came packing in, one thousand men, women, and animals on double-length railroad cars, and out came the marching advertisement, the free street parade.

Plumed horses, all color and light, drew the ornate gold-and-red lead wagon, and the windjammer band played a wild, disparate repertoire punched by a pair of great cymbals and a big bass drum. Circus wagons went past with a hollow truckling sound, and clowns ran all about tossing hard candy as freely as the old-time Uncle Sam clown, Dan Rice, had tossed money from a hat before the War.

Hundreds and hundreds flooded into Elizabeth City from the countryside to laugh and point and drink and fight, but above all to see the fine horseflesh and woman-flesh that was all sparkles and molded silk from where they sat in the bleachers. To see the boat racing and to bet the ponies, the runners and the fast trotters Little Jack, Yazoo, Dr. SK. To gaze upon the wonders of the world: the Garsenneti acrobat family from South America, the Martells with their fancy trick bicycles, Madam Marantette and her jumping horses, the female Zouave corps in a bewildering military drill, and the Bloody Sixth Rough Riders just in from their victories in the Philippines.

That year a restless, tethered horse kicked a twelve-year-old boy named Morris Bright in the head and killed him. The circus workers drank and fought over each other's husbands and wives and occasionally went after each other with tent stakes and knives.

It was the Walter L. Main Grandest and Best Show on Earth from Trumbull, Ohio.

JIM WILCOX

I went into Hathaway's on the second circus day and ordered some tickets.

—What's it cost?

—Fifty cents, children a quarter.

—How much does it get you?

—All the way through the menagerie, the hippo-drome, the three-ring circus, and the Rough Rider exhi-bition.

I ordered two and asked for em to be sent around to the Cropseys, one for Carrie, one for Nell.

OLLIE CROPSEY

I know one of the reasons they argued was all the pro-hibition talk after Reverend Stuart left Elizabeth City. After all, the Wilcoxes were Republicans and Republi-cans had fought prohibition for years. But Papa said with the grandfather clause the Negroes couldn't vote and they always voted Republican, so finally the Demo-crats could get prohibition through. We Cropseys were good Democrats, so it was no wonder Nell and Jim fought.

Nellie was tired of him, too. She wasn't nearly as im-pressed with him as she'd been when we moved down and she was getting all the attentions of the sheriff's son. Now she was short with him and that was unlike her.

But when the circus came she got a little friendlier with him again. Jim met us at Seven Pines after he got off work at the shipyards, and the four of us—Jim, Nell, Carrie, and I—strolled over to the fairgrounds after the first-day crowds had gone home.

We walked along the midway where there were paint-ed backdrops of darky minstrels and exotic animals and women barely dressed, and we stopped at a set of scales where the man would guess your weight.

Nell weighed a hundred and ten—Hunnert'n'ten, the man said.

The next morning a boy brought an envelope to the house with circus tickets for Nell and Carrie from Jim. He didn't send me any and I can't recall if he knew Papa had already given me one or not. Jim couldn't go because of his work, so we three girls went.

We saw an automobile operated.

And the equestriennes who posed and pirouetted and leapt and somersaulted—they were beautiful! For a moment I thought we were home and had gone to Madison Square Garden. Carrie said all the riding horses were white or dappled so the powdered resin wouldn't show. The horses had to have resin on their backs or else the riders would slip from their perspiration.

Papa told us all the talk he heard around town was saloons or no saloons. That, and so many were mad about the new president who invited Booker T. Washington, a Negro, to eat with him at the White House. That was Roosevelt, who was a Republican.

One evening in early November, Jim was taking his hat to go home and Nell said *Pull* to him real sharply. Pull was what you told your horse to hurry him up. She went to the door with him but didn't stay even a minute. After that she never saw him to the door and never went out with him except with Carrie along, too. Carrie walked between them and I noticed that now Nell and Jim never spoke.

Saturday, a week before she was going to leave, Jim asked Nellie and me to go sailing with him but we said no. Instead he took Carrie and Let, one of my older sisters. He got them lunch at a restaurant and then kept them out in the boat till late—not late like he had with Nell those times, but late into the dusk, near six. We were all uneasy, and when they did get back, Let said that Jim had wanted to wrap her in a blanket and bring her into the house as if she were dead, just to frighten Mama.

It's no wonder we've never believed Jim Wilcox.

He made a date to take Carrie out to Munden's Roller Skating Rink down on Water Street. I suppose he meant to spite Nell. When he came for Carrie, it was Tuesday evening. Nell would only be with us one more day. We were in the living room dancing to Uncle Hen's mouth-harp music. We knew it was Jim's ring. We had one of those twistbells that was built into the door, and Jim always rang the same way.

Nell asked me to let him in, but I wouldn't.

—Girls, Carrie said, I'm tired of rude manners.

She answered the door and found Jim nervous and awkward. He told Carrie to get her hat and they'd go. While Carrie went for her things, he tried to talk with Nell by asking her how the corn on her foot was, saying he supposed it was getting better.

Nell wouldn't look at him, but she turned my way and smiled a bit at me and said, A little.

After they left she told me I ought to go and see what they did, so I asked Uncle Hen to take me to the rink. We arrived as Jim and Carrie were just putting on their skates. It was very loud in there, that big empty room echoing the sound of the skate wheels hitting the wood floor and the ballbearing sound of the spinning wheels when someone fell.

One of Jim's sisters skated by, and he remarked very sarcastically, They call that my sister. I haven't spoken to her for two years. And I told him he ought to be ashamed.

Uncle Hen and I got home first because Jim and Carrie went off down Poindexter looking for some fruit. Nell was writing a letter at the dining room table, and when Jim came in the house he tapped me on the shoulder and motioned at Nell without saying anything as if he wanted to know whom she was so busy writing.

—I certainly would enjoy a good apple, Nell looked up and said.

Carrie passed the fruit around. Jim and I both took some, but Nellie, when she realized that Jim had bought it, refused. Soon after that, Carrie walked him to the door and when she returned, Nell was busily eating one of the apples.

—Nell, I nearly laughed when you refused the apple that cool way—I knew you really wanted one.

—It was a good joke on Jim, Nell said.

—I told him what you said about him this afternoon, about having no more use for him, Carrie said.

—How'd he take it?

—Never said a word to me till we got near the house. Then he started in, but I reminded him how he'd been acting. You should have seen us going to the rink. I felt like an elephant with that little thing—I'm so much taller than he is.

—Why don't you call him Squatty? Nell said, and we all had a laugh on that. After we'd gotten the cups and saucers and dishes out and set the table for breakfast, we went on up to bed.

That was the night before Nell disappeared.

LEN OWENS

—Damn it, we're late, the Captain said.

The smack *Ray* pulled out of Shallowbag Bay, Manteo, sometime between nine and ten Wednesday morning, November 20th, 1901, bound for Elizabeth City. The crew was Captain Bailey and Len Owens the engineer and Sherman Tillet the black mate. That was all.

They didn't clear the Nags Head soundside landing till around noon, and by then the wind was kicking up so they used their sails rather than the engine. They made three trips a week back and forth, and there was one more stop, Powell's Point at the mouth of the North River. Then they took the *Ray* on into Elizabeth City.

—We'll be lucky to make town by midnight, Captain Bailey said.

But they did, and by doing so Len Owens became a crucial witness, witness to a mystery, before that night was out.

JIM WILCOX

There's more pretty girls than one, the song says.

Least Carrie was nice and civil to me and I didn't mind at all thinking I might make Nell jealous taking Carrie out. When we walked back from the rink that night she told me Nell pretty much couldn't stand me anymore.

—Why is it Nell dislikes you so, Jim? she asked me.

I told her Nell didn't even care enough for me to see me to the door and I'd decided to drop her.

—You mean she'll drop *you*, Carrie said.

That was about the size of it. That business about the apple burned me up. Then on my way out I stopped to light a cigaret between the front door and the vestibule door and I heard em laughing at me. I could hear em through the broken pane.

Next day I walked over to Mister Fearing's stable after I finished up work and met Carrie and Let there. I told Carrie that listeners never heard any good of themselves and she apologized.

—Why didn't you come unharness the horse for us?

Let laughed at me. Well, boy, I been lackey long enough and I told her so. I was going to have a word with Nell Cropsey before she left if it killed me. Three-and-a-half years I spent on her or wasted on her one. I'm going to tell her good-bye for good before she goes to New York, I thought. We went over to the Cropsey house and stood around the kitchen talking a bit. Nellie was sitting in front of a looking glass and ignoring me as usual. I slapped Ollie on the back and let her know what a nice girl I thought she was for joking about me like she had the night before. Then Nell hopped up, acting cute, talking about what fun she and Carrie'd have on the steamer that coming Saturday, Nell playing harmonica and Carrie on mandolin and them passing the hat for coins.

I didn't pay any attention to her. I was going to say my good-byes later on.

There's more pretty girls than one.

CALE PARKER

It was sunset time that night. The thin iceclouds were high in the sky, and the long sunrays stretched over the flatlands and wide waters, the lightlines longer and thinner till at last the long lines softened, lost their tension, and disintegrated, and dusk fell on the Pasquotank. The moon was already rising in the cold November sky, enough to light the pineywoods and the county roads cut through them.

About that time, a little man named Cale Parker fed and hitched his horse, making ready to leave his Frog Island farm in south Pasquotank and get on back to Elizabeth City, eleven miles to the north.

Cale Parker drove along at a jog, maybe five or six

miles an hour, he reckoned. Won't no hurry. He made the Sawyer-Meads store five miles from his farm between seven and eight, and he stopped to rest the horse but mostly to jaw.

—Whatdya say, Cale?

—Boys.

—Fellow raises hogs an' hominy, now he's all right.

—You heard about the 'leven cent cotton?

—Naw, but I heard all I care to about the four cent.

—Believe if I had me a wife on a cold night like this I'd be gettin on home to her, Cale.

—Hell, the rate he's gettin there we liable to find him an' the hoss an' buggy all froze to the road in the morning.

—Be seein you, boys.

—Be seein you, Cale.

Cale Parker had stopped to rest his horse, but mostly to jaw and get warm and now, after an hour or more, he was done there, so he drove on toward Mack Fletcher's store up the road, where he could do it all again.

The silent witness, the bright waxing Beaver Moon, rose higher in the cold sky. The moment was coming.

Hell, his wife didn't care when he got home. So Cale stopped again when he reached Fletcher's store and went inside, where he stayed another hour.

—What time is it got to be?

—Ten, thereabouts.

—I'd of been home now if I hadn't of stopped.

Cale Parker talked another ten or fifteen minutes and then headed on toward town at the same steady gait. He stopped at bridges and muddy places and walked his horse and buggy over them so the thin wheels wouldn't mire. The hard cold was setting, but the mudholes weren't frozen yet. It was too damn cold to get stuck.

Now Cale could put away some liquor, that was no secret. He'd drink and pass out in the buggy and trust his
good horse to pull him in that buggy all the way home to
where his wife would hear the clanking of the hames and
buckles and come outside. The horse, with Cale dead
drunk in tow, would have stopped at the gate, waiting.
She'd get up and open the gate and let them in and prod
her reeking man into the house and bed.

But Cale Parker swore he wasn't drinking that night.

Five miles up the road from Fletcher's he reached the
Cropsey house, Cropsey the potato trucker down from
New York with all the young'uns.

Who was that he saw there?

A man and a woman about the same height were
walking along the side of the road. Maybe a boy and a
girl. Medium-size people. Cale noticed heights because
he was barely five feet tall. It looked like the man was
the size of the woman. He couldn't see the man's face.
Well, it could of been anybody—he met a lot of people
walking on the rivershore road.

The boys at Fletcher's store told Cale it was about ten,
and he stayed on a bit. If he left at ten or before, Cale
Parker missed the moment of Nell Cropsey's disappearance. But if he left after ten, then he should have been
passing the Cropsey house between eleven and quarter
past.

It could have happened either way.

Then Cale Parker saw another man walking just a little way behind the couple. Just a little way back. Who
was it? Nobody was saying nothing to nobody. There was
just the clanking of the hames and buckles and the thin
wheels on the hard ground and the wind soughing
through the cypress and pines and blowing the clouds
across the moon.

OLLIE CROPSEY

He was hateful that last day. In the afternoon he came in the kitchen with Let and Carrie, popped me hard on the back, and said sarcastically, You're a nice girl, and I knew right away he'd overheard us laughing at him. Before he left he rubbed soot across Carrie's face and my face. I grabbed a corncob and ran it over the stove-top and poked the sooty thing at Jim to pay him back. He ran out the back door, never saying good-bye or anything. I wish to God he had never returned.

I had rarely seen Nell in such high spirits. Uncle Hen blew a few tunes on the harp while she and I danced our way in to the supper table while Nell sang out,

> Here I go with my lame foot,
> Come on dance with me.

She still had her toe taped up and bandaged on account of the trouble that corn was giving her.

Eight or eight-thirty Jim came back. Nell and Carrie sat at the dining room table sewing jackets for their trip. Roy Crawford was there, but he and Jim never spoke. I said hello to Jim twice before he'd even reply.

Our parents went up to bed soon, and Uncle Hen would've too, but Nell pouted and cajoled him to play more songs. When he quit she told him he was stingy with his wind. She couldn't get enough music.

Jim sat in a rocker between the corner stove and the door from the dining room to the hallway. After a while, he asked me if there was any water in the pump, and I said I guessed there was a little and handed him a glass. He wouldn't take it.

—I might poison it, he said.

Jim was stiff and cold and gruff all night. He sat in

the rocker and every now and again checked his pocket watch. He stared off into space and didn't pay one whit of attention to our conversation. Nellie and Roy wouldn't bother with him, and I didn't feel like it myself.

—Jim! Carrie said suddenly. What are you smiling about?

At least Carrie would be a little nice to him. I couldn't wait for Nell and Carrie to be gone so Jim wouldn't come around anymore. He was too much to bear like this.

—Was I smiling? he asked. I didn't know it.

She managed to coax him into a conversation and they somehow got to talking about death.

—I nearly drowned one time, he said. There was a very pleasant sensation in my head. That's how I want to die.

The rest of us stopped talking and looked up at Jim and Carrie.

—I'd want to drown in my favorite pond, she said. Near where we live in New York.

Since Carrie had spoken, Nell felt free to. She still hadn't said a word directly to Jim since the night she told him, Pull.

—Well, I wouldn't want to drown and have my hair come all out of its crimps, Nell said. I'd want to freeze— that's about the easiest way to die.

Jim checked his pocket watch again, and I looked up at the clock. I certainly didn't want to think about dying or suicide. Carrie started up for bed three times, but Nell pleaded with her so to stay a little longer that each time she came back for a few minutes.

—Don't go, Nell said and sang, You'll miss me when I'm gone! Carrie sat on Nell's lap and didn't go upstairs to bed till about quarter to eleven.

We all stood when Carrie finally left the room, and Roy Crawford chucked Nell under the chin, saying, Nell, you look mighty sweet tonight.

And I said, As if she didn't always look so.

Jim said nothing and sat like the bump on the log he'd been most of the night, until he checked his pocket watch one last time.

—Eleven o'clock. My mama said I must be in at eleven tonight.

—My, but you're getting good, Jim, I said.

He rolled a cigaret. I remember that, and then he took his hat from the finial of the rocker and walked out into the hall, whereupon he turned and looked back through the door and spoke:

—Nell, can I see you out here a minute?

I'll never forget that moment. He spoke and Nell, not answering, looked at me quizzically. When I die, I pray I meet our Lord, that I might ask Him and learn why He let me nod yes to Nell my beloved sister, and why He let me close the door behind her forever.

LEN OWENS

The *Ray* made it up into the Pasquotank River before the winds dropped off. They were abreast of Newlen Creek about 10:30 when the Captain said to take in the sails, so Len and Sherman set to it.

Len fired the engine and Captain Bailey said, Well, we'll probably make five miles an hour on into town. It was still windy, but in gusts now so they couldn't depend on it. After they made the moorings at the Norfolk and Southern depot wharf, the Captain looked down at his hanging clock in the cabin and said:

—Half past eleven exactly. Len, I want you to stop to

the bar and buy me half a pint. You go along with him, Sherman, and bring it back to me.

The Captain jumped into the cabin and put water on the stove. He wouldn't be doing without his hot whiskey on a cold night like this.

Len Owens and Sherman Tillet trotted along with their hands in their pockets, it was that cold. They made Barnes's bar by the Poindexter Creek bridge in maybe five minutes. No one was there but Barnes and his boy.

—Bring a bottle with you? Barnes asked.

Len hadn't, so Barnes rinsed one out and filled it from a barreltap.

—Some cigarets, too, Owens said. He took off the silver paper they came in, lit a smoke, and gave one to Sherman along with the bottle. Another five minutes elapsed in the bar before they left.

Len Owens walked double quick along Poindexter Street, put his cold, cold hands in his pockets, and trotted to the short bridge over Tiber Creek. There was not a soul abroad till he crossed the Charles Creek bridge over to Dry Point, where he saw Jim Wilcox coming at him in the moonlight.

—Hello, old boy, Jim said to him. Owens had been knowing the ex-sheriff's boy a fair while. He seemed right genial and at ease in spite of the bitter cold. He rolled a cigaret, and Len had one of his storeboughts.

—Where you been keeping yourself, Len?

—Coming and going, three trips a week. Hard winds and bad weather lately. Been to see your girl?

—Yeah, Jim Wilcox said.

It was too cold for much of that, so they split off, each heading to his own home. Len Owens bet himself that the bilge-pump water on the deck of the *Ray* was probably freezing. He called his wife from the front porch of his Morgan Street house four or five times before she woke up and let him in. He'd been out on the water all day, and Lord, he had a bone-deep chill.

They locked the door and went upstairs, and Len heard the tolling of the courthouse bell as he undressed. Way across the black river, the steam whistle blew at Blades's shingle mill and the night-force men stopped for midnight lunch.

A hard winter cold set its grip upon the low tidelands and all the sound country. Men out on boats drank hot whiskey to stay alive, while a waxing moon rose and fell and dark clouds passed by and mill workers cut shingles in the night. Bells and whistles sounded through the brittle cold-snap night that froze that black river to its edges. Nell Cropsey vanished and the moment froze clear through.

THE TRIAL

W. O. SAUNDERS

On a cold, sunny Friday morning two days after Christmas 1901, a couple of fishermen out on the Pasquotank saw something dark floating in the river less than a hundred yards away.

—What's that? one of them started.

—A log?

—A piece of old boat hull?

They paddled over to where they could get a better look.

It was a woman's body, floating face down, her loose tresses waving at length on the river's surface. They dared not touch her—one of them ran an oar down into the soft ooze of the river bottom to mark the spot, and then they rowed straight in to the sandy beach in front of the house the Cropseys called Seven Pines.

William Cropsey's wife, weeping hysterically, met them at the shore.

Nell Cropsey was found.

OLLIE CROPSEY

I heard Mama shriek and run out front and down to the river where the rowboat was making its way in. They found her, they found her, she was screaming.

Papa put on his heavy coat and went with the two men, who kept apologizing and saying maybe it's not her, maybe it's just not. We didn't touch her, they said— didn't see her face. It could be anyone, but you'd best come with us, Mister Cropsey.

It is like a dream that never leaves me.

Mama is at the edge of the river sobbing Nell, my Nell, and we try to get her back into the house where at least it is warm. Papa climbs into the rowboat, and one of the men tells a little boy to go and fetch the coroner— go and tell Doctor Ike there's a dead girl in the river. And Papa says nothing. The oarlocks creak against the wood as the boat goes out. We walk Mama slowly back to the house, and I turn to look out on the river as the boat stops by some sort of stake. I can see one of the men— it must be Papa—reaching his arms into the water and taking hold of her and turning her round to see, and I look away.

Then we are in the house and there is ringing in my ears and a tight hard knot in my breast and I am taking shorter and shorter breaths. I hear voices and see out the window that people are gathering, though I can barely focus on them or on Papa getting out of the boat and walking up to the porch. Then he comes into the living room and says,

—It's Nell.

I do not awaken from this dream.

When it turned warm again, I got in the habit of swimming the quarter mile from our house up the river to the wharf at the foot of Main Street. Many is the time I made that swim with a prayer in my heart—Lord, forgive me, for I put her in this black river with a nod.

TALK

Word flew through the river town like an indiscreet coupling of magic and wildfire, and hundreds from every walk of life left their tasks and swarmed down by the river that was the lifeblood of their town, the dark river that had at last given up its dead beauty, Nell Cropsey.

—Who found her?

—J. D. Stillman—he'll get a hundred dollars for it.

—She drowned?

—Don't know yet—they're waiting on the coroner.

All morning and the rest of the day, men from the swamp country headed for Elizabeth City as the word got around that they'd found Nell Cropsey dead in the Pasquotank River.

—I never heard of a drowned woman floating face down.

—Me neither.

—How'd she look?

—I heard she was just as good looking as ever. That was a pretty gal, boy.

—I thought maybe the crabs and fish might of got at her. You know how they do.

The liquor was flowing that day, and the town's bar-rooms were doing land-office business. Crowds spilled out of the saloons, onto street corners, by the wharves. And everywhere they formed, there were threats against the life of Jim Wilcox.

—Where's that son of a bitch Wilcox?

—Deputy Reid's gone down the county to Newbegun to get him.

—What about the girl, now, what'd you say?

—Well, I understood em to say she's a looker even dead and been in the river all this time.

—How you know she's *been* in the river all this time? Reckon she's a pure virgin?

—Don't know. Waiting on the coroner about that too. They're supposed to be looking her over down at the Cropsey house. You want to go?

—Let's have us another round first.

The word spread and the liquor flowed and the talk got rougher as the day went on. They were working the mob beast up to its task, the simple duty of getting drunk and coiling a rope and throwing it over a limb and putting Jim Wilcox's neck in the noose and seeing Judge Lynch's justice done up proper.

The Autopsy (Morning)

Doctor Ike Fearing drove up in his buggy just as the fishermen were coming back in with William Cropsey. Cropsey had identified his daughter, and they had tied her body to the oar-stob before rowing in again to get the coroner.

So this was Nell Cropsey, lifeless in the Pasquotank River, after thirty-seven days of anguish, vigil, search, and suspicion. How had she eluded them—all that dragging, cannon firing, the diver, and the electric submarine lantern? She seemed amazingly well preserved, only a bit swollen and her skin slightly tinted from so much time in the dark juniper water.

The coroner held the rope that was tied to her arm and they towed Nell Cropsey in to shore. At the sandy beach, they pulled her from the water, wrapped her in a sheet, and placed her on a quilt. A few men stepped forward from the swelling crowd and, pulling the quilt taut like a stretcher, carried her up to one of the outbuildings, a windowless barn in back of the house on the west side.

Doctor Ike sent for a couple more physicians and empaneled a six-man coroner's jury. About eleven o'clock, they proceeded to conduct the inquest in that crude working room.

The big barn doors had to be thrown wide open in order for there to be enough light. Chief Dawson and his men formed a police line to keep the ever-growing crowd back from the barn. The gawking mob pressed in as close as it could—everyone wanted to see Beautiful Nell Cropsey.

She lay on a makeshift table with her feet toward the open doors. Except for a missing slipper, her clothing seemed to be in no disarray. There was a small bandage tied around one of her toes, covering the corn that Jim Wilcox had asked about six weeks before. The doctors and the coroner's jurymen looked for the photographs Wilcox claimed he'd returned at that last meeting, but they found nothing. Then, in short order, they did something that set the crowd on edge.

They stripped her naked.

Right in front of two thousand people they stripped her all the way down except for a pair of black stockings. Only those in the first two or three rows could see, but they turned and told and the words cut like a knife through the mob—them boys up front can see every bit of her! There were adolescent boys and plenty of men a good deal older seeing their first naked woman. There were blacks looking on, too, but the white men were too busy staring themselves to care that niggers were getting an eyeful of white womanflesh. All morning and all afternoon, men jostled their way up to the police line and once there—Jesus, you could see everything!

To all appearances, Doctor Ike said, there were no external injuries. Then he took his scalpel and made a neat vertical incision from just below the breastbone down to the pubic bone. He cut her wide open.

There was no water in her stomach.

Her lungs were collapsed and empty, except for a small bit of bloody fluid. Doctor Ike cut off a piece of lung and pressed it between his hands—a froth oozed out. He dropped it in a jar of water and said,

—It floats.

Both chambers of her heart were empty.

The jurymen shifted from foot to foot, uneasy, uncertain. What did it mean? A stenographer took it all down. Doc, what about—?

The coroner lifted out the female organs.

—She was a virgin, he said.

That would quiet the gossips. Death would have been God's just punishment had she been pregnant or unchaste, but now, all the more righteous indignation could come down on Jim Wilcox.

The three doctors worked on her torso while the jurymen were gathered at her feet. One of them, Ferebee the barber, looked up the length of the dead girl's body and, after an undertone conversation with the other jurors, ventured,

—Doesn't her head look a little fuller on the one side? Ferebee was pointing to a swelling of the left temple.

—It's a dropsical form of flesh, one of the doctors said. Being in the water caused it. She's swollen all over, look.

He then put his finger on the nipple of Nell Cropsey's left breast and pressed it down. Those who saw were startled—a nervous snigger ran through the crowd, belying both shame and fascination. It was done by a doctor, surely he had the right.

—But there's a great deal more flesh there than on the head, said Ferebee the barber.

—Well, *you* do it then, said the doctor.

Ferebee pressed his finger on her left temple and his touch there left an indentation. Then he, too, put his finger on her nipple and pressed down on her breast just as the doctor had done and with the doctor's sanction.

—Good deal of difference, the barber said.

By that time they had been at their grim task for several hours—ten men in a windowless barn on a cold, sunny day just past Christmas '01, cutting apart the body of Beautiful Nell Cropsey, who lay stripped naked on a slab table as two thousand people strained to see.

Chief Dawson closed the barn doors.

The ten men went for lunch.

JIM WILCOX

I was out laying for ducks. I was down gunning in south Pasquotank when they come out and got me. Deputy Reid called to me across the field and when I got over to him he told me what was what.

—She's dead, Jim. Stillman and Long found her this morning in the river. I got to take you in.

We got on his buckboard and started for town, and I was right scared, knowing we'd be going by the Cropsey house. Deputy Reid said there was a crowd and the town was riled up but good. I hated to leave the country, the way things were running against me in town.

I've kept on coming down to the south of the county to lay low and stay out of the way. Right when Hoover went out last year, Kelly Tillet and his wife Sudie gave me a room and I stayed on down there a while. Kelly and me fished out of his fish camp at Frog Island there where Big Flatty runs into Albemarle Sound.

They made me feel right comfortable. I don't know what I'd of done without Kelly and Sudie and the rest. Their daughter married Charlie Eves who always bought me packs of Bull Durhams that we'd sit and roll. My mama was Mattie Eves, and all those Eves were kin to me. The first one in Pasquotank was a Union soldier who come back to live after the War, and there's Eveses there yet.

My cough was getting worse but it weren't a bad time last fall. We played checkers and I worked crossword puzzles in the newspapers. Pearce Eves even learned how to work that solid brass puzzle lock I'd made in prison. There were a lot of squirrels, so me and some of the younger ones'd go out squirreling. They were all good to me. I could come and go down there as I pleased and nobody asked questions.

I was real taken with Kelly and Sudie's baby girl Roselyn. I made her a rattan sort of bedstead out of vines from the woods, and once I tied a sucker to a string and swung it in front of her and told her I'd let her have it if she'd say Jim Wilcox. I wanted to hear her call my name, but all she could say was Coocox, Coocox, bless her heart. I told Sudie when I die bury me under the pear tree out front of the house so my ghost could watch over that little girl.

One evening I went to Charlie Eves's house where he and Ethelyn was picking May peas on the porch. I was aching bad to talk. Charlie and me went out and sat under the apple trees.

—They say I killed that girl, Charlie.

—Course you didn't, Jim.

—I think I know who did. When I was up at Central, somebody come to see me, come in when I was polishing up the electric chair. I told him the man that killed Nell Cropsey was walking the streets of Elizabeth City that very minute with money in his pocket. If I could just get a little time with Ollie, but they keep her locked up and won't let me get to her.

—You know, Jim, a lot of folks think her old man did it.

I'd heard that story, but I didn't say so. I wanted to hear it the way it'd come down to Charlie Eves. So I let him finish.

Then we come in from the apple trees and I went on my way—that weren't all so very long ago. All my cousins and kin down there been good to me. Most of em weren't even born that day when Deputy Reid arrested me—for *abduction* he said.

—Well, now, Jim. Aren't you a handsome fellow for a girl to go and drown herself over?

That was a queer thing for him to say, and so I kind of laughed and said,

—Ain't I, though?

Boy, let me tell you there was trouble in town when we got there. Elizabeth City has just plain had it in for me all my life.

THE AUTOPSY (AFTERNOON)

Ferebee the barber and the other coroner's jurymen, upset over what they had seen and not understood, went to see Solicitor Ward during the lunch break and told him there was a bump on Nell Cropsey's head and what did he think?

The solicitor went straight to Doctor Ike and wanted to know if she'd drowned or was it murder? Hard to say. They'd seen no external injuries, but there was no water in her lungs either. Maybe he'd better have another look. The coroner rounded up his examiners and they all returned to the Cropsey barn between three and four that afternoon. The crowds opened a path for the men who were determined to clear this thing up for once and all.

—We got to get more light on that head.

—Turn her on around so her head's up by the door.

As they shifted the body, several of the long dark curls fell out. One of the jurymen carefully removed the rest a handful at a time. They noticed again how the top layer of her skin was loose and slid like an oiled cloth over a gun barrel.

Doctor Ike cut all the way around her scalp.

When his scalpel struck her left temple, about a tablespoon of thick, black blood oozed out. The men leaned in closer. He removed her scalp. They could plainly see a round, bluish-tinged bruise a little larger than a silver dollar.

He sawed through her skull and took the top of her head off. The decayed brain ran out like pus, and the men reeled back from the table and the immediate, unbearable stench in that airless barn.

—That settles it, said one of the doctors, and Nell Cropsey's rough passage from this world was ended.

The remains lay slit open, the vitals exposed and the head half cut away, and she was naked yet but for the black silk stockings. Next to her lay her dark brown curls all in a pile. The two thousand onlookers were still there. The doctors would, of course, put her back together for burying. Then they and the jurymen would retire and reach a verdict.

The inquest was over.

W. O. SAUNDERS

I've known this town right well for a long time now, and if there was ever a time when it was out and out berserk, it was that weekend after they found Nell Cropsey.

Then and during Jim's trial.

Though for a while there, it didn't look like he was going to need a trial, there were so many anxious citizens bent on saving the state the trouble and money.

When Deputy Reid brought Jim in from the country, the wagon had to go right smack through the crowd that was milling around enjoying the autopsy Doctor Isaiah Fearing was holding there on the Cropsey property. Apparently the air was thick with threats against him, and they could have easily gotten him then. But that particular crowd was so possessed by its psychosexual interest in the course of the autopsy that Jim was more a distraction than a main feature.

Not so with the drunk gangs downtown. Our town had filled up with rabble. Country boys and country men had come into town to drink and find a target for the fume and rage left in their guts by a failed crop or a dead mule or bad whiskey or a cold woman.

Deputy Reid drove the wagon through the muttering

crowds and carried Jim across town to the mayor's office. It must have been one hell of a harrowing ride for that pair.

There was open talk in the streets for lynching Jim Wilcox that very night, and the county sheriff expected trouble. He wired the governor at four P.M.:

Miss Cropsey found in river. Threats of violence against Wilcox. Notify naval reserves to be at my command.

N. G. Grandy, Sheriff

At seven the return wire came from Raleigh:

Your telegram received. Naval reserves ordered to obey your orders. Maintain the law at all hazards. Keep me fully informed by wire.

C. B. Aycock, Governor

The huge fire alarm bell atop the firehouse rang out, calling out the reserves to protect the most roundly despised man in all Pasquotank. Within minutes picket lines were stationed, and the Third Division, Naval Battalion, North Carolina State Guard, known locally as the Pasquotank Rifles, bivouacked that night beneath the pecan trees in the courthouse square.

The Rifles, who had won a gold medal at the 1896 Edenton fair for best-drilled corps, were rattled. The alert had come so fast that no one had had time to get into uniform. And there was a fear abroad among them as they felt the confused hurt of suddenly finding themselves at blood odds with their friends and neighbors.

The mayor ordered the bars shut down.

Nell Cropsey's body was placed in a metal casket and, after nightfall, stored in a vault in the old Episcopal cemetery not far from the Wilcox home. Doctor Ike and his coroner's jury moved to the Academy of Music to deliberate.

And at seven-thirty, this telegram went to the governor:

All quiet now. Jury has not yet returned a verdict.

N. G. Grandy, Sheriff

Friday, December 27th, 1901, was a wild day for Elizabeth City, and it was not over yet.

TALK

The bars were closed, but there was no shortage of liquor for the gangs that were roaming the streets. There were gruesome rumors abroad about Nell Cropsey.

—Her neck was broke.

—The crabs and fish eat up her flesh something awful.

—I hear they got her over in the Pool family vault.

—Let's go have a look.

Spurred by whiskey and morbidity, the drunk mob barged into the Episcopal cemetery and trampled through gravestones, cold December slabs in the torchlight, and they searched vault to vault.

—Hell, it's locked.

—What?

—The damn vault's locked.

—Maybe she ain't here.

—That's right. Maybe they carried her back over to her folks' place. That's what they'd do, ain't it? So they could be with her just these last days?

—When's the burying?

—Funeral was supposed to be tomorrow at five. The doctors kept examining so long they moved it back to

Sunday at two. Don't know anything about the burying.

—What if she's over at the house? You think we—

—No.

—Hell.

W. O. SAUNDERS

Doctor Ike and the others agreed in secret session that the town was too heated up to take their report, and they decided to wait till morning to release it. There was already some garbled report circulating, and Doctor Ike wasn't about to play into the hands of the mob. Finally the gangs broke up and went home.

It was a shrewd move, and I think I'd have done the same thing had I been in Doctor Ike's place.

But Saturday was market day, and Elizabeth City was full to brimming again. Curious farmers and their families massed outside the Academy of Music, along with the hotheads from the previous night. They quieted to hear the report read. I saved the clipping that quotes it verbatim:

We, the coroner's jury, having been duly summoned and sworn by Dr. I. Fearing to inquire what caused the death of Ella M. Cropsey, do hereby report, from the investigation made by three physicians of Elizabeth City, and from their opinion and also from our personal observation, that said Ella M. Cropsey came to her death by being stricken a blow on the left temple and by being drowned in the Pasquotank River.

We have not yet investigated nor heard any testimony touching as to who inflicted the blow and did the drowning. We are informed that one James Wilcox is charged with same, and is now in custody. We recommend that investigation as to his or any one else's probable guilt be had by one or more magistrates in Elizabeth City township, and that said Wilcox be held to await said investigation.

> I. Fearing, M.D., Coroner
> B. F. Spence
> Robert J. Mitchell
> J. H. LeRoy
> P. S. Shipp
> Maurice Wescott
> J. B. Ferebee

Their actually naming Jim Wilcox fascinated me— they were in effect using the report as a surrogate indictment. No one would try a thing like that nowadays, but back then it wasn't questioned. To me it reflects the extent to which the town had made this one strange case into a crusade almost from the beginning. Why this time? It seemed as accidental, as passionate, and every bit as unpredictable as a love affair, which in a way it was. The death of a beautiful young woman, Poe once wrote, is the most poetical topic in the world.

Everyone who heard the coroner's report had his or her worst angry suspicions confirmed. It was murder, they said, and it was Wilcox that did it.

Again there were open expressions against Jim at every turn. There was the constant reminder of black crepe bunting draped in the store windows and on office doors. There were the militiamen, standing guard out of uniform, but with Winchesters and pistols loaded.

As for Jim Wilcox, he occupied the top half of the two-story steel jail cage, having the run of four adjoining cells there, while six Negroes huddled in the bottom and wondered whether they too might get caught in the lynch wrath that could easily carry all before it. There were laws against the practice on North Carolina books, but, at the time, no lyncher in the state had ever been punished.

They say Jim was indifferent and unconcerned, that even as armed guards kept the crowds a block back from the jail, he said to one militiaman,

—You might as well go on home. I ain't afraid of a lynching.

I'd say Jim Wilcox has been one of the most talked-about people in this town. And I wouldn't be so sure he was as cool as all that, however bluff he may have tried to act.

His sister Sadie paid him a visit that Saturday afternoon and spent a half hour telling him about the coroner's verdict and how the town was more worked up than ever. When she left, tears streaming down her face, he was shook and nervous.

The local solicitor, George Ward, was already putting together what he must have known was a circumstantial murder case against Jim. He told the press that he feared the mob was heating up again and that Jim might not last the night. He noted that though the bars remained closed, there was a lot of drinking going on and a seemingly constant supply of liquor. The crowds were growing more aggressive and truculent. Solicitor Ward looked out on the town that had elected him and said,

—All that mob needs is a leader.

OLLIE CROPSEY

Papa was upset and angered by the coroner's report. He thought it went much too easy on Jim. The evidence was strong against him, but it was still hard to believe he would hurt Nell. That he would *kill* her. They had been sweethearts so long. But it's true, he didn't so much as lift a finger to help find her. Papa asked the Committee to take over the arrangements for Nell's funeral. None of us had strength enough to face that.

The night before the funeral, a great crowd of men came to Seven Pines and called Papa out on the front porch. They told him they were going after Jim Wilcox with a rope. They said they had friends and supporters among the reserves and deputies who guarded Jim, and that these would stand aside or even join them when the time came. Once they got Jim out of jail they would hang him from the nearest stout tree.

They wanted Papa to lead them.

Papa said no.

He said no and thanked them and told them to let the law take its course. Though no one wanted to see justice done so much as we Cropseys, he would not join them in this lawless act.

So many, many times Papa has wished, not that he had led them, but that he had simply nodded yes. They were in such a fever, he said, and they would have torn the jail apart to get at Jim.

To me, one of the queerest things about the whole tragic affair is this: on the day the coroner's verdict practically indicted Jim, the night before poor Nell's funeral, my father stood out on the porch where Jim may well have killed her and told the lynch mob no.

My father saved Jim Wilcox's life.

The Funeral

The Methodist Church bell began to toll the moment the undertakers carried Nell Cropsey's casket from Seven Pines, placed it in a rubber-tired hearse, and drove off. Jim Wilcox heard the bell and asked his jailer if there was going to be much of a crowd at the funeral.

Despite an intermittent, driving rain from the winter storm that had kicked up, fifteen hundred people assembled in the Methodist Church, and hundreds more lined Church Street on either side.

They took off their hats when the hearse arrived and the pallbearers, the Committee men, lifted the black walnut casket from the hearse. Weeping in the church increased as they bore the black box down the center aisle. Beneath the three green-and-white sprays, where none could see, was a small inscription, *At Rest*.

The bell stopped tolling.

One of the ministers cautioned the congregation to hold its judgment of Jim Wilcox. Be guided, he said, to a peace and equanimity beyond this moment.

—Deliver me, O Lord, from the evil man; Preserve me from the violent man. He read from the Hundred-fortieth Psalm, then spoke again of Jim Wilcox.

—I believe him innocent of the dark charge which hangs over him.

A wave of disapproval went through the church, whispers and talk. They would not hear of it. They sang:

> Abide with me, fast falls the eventide;
> The darkness deepens, Lord with me abide!

Then came the Methodist minister, Devil-Hunter Tuttle he was called, said to be so uncompromising and strict that he wouldn't let his wife so much as heat gravy on Sundays.

—A sad and mysterious Providence has come to a home in our community, Tuttle began.

—We thank God the family has been sustained in their sorrow.

> When other helpers fail and comforts flee,
> Help of the helpless, O abide with me.

—We thank Thee she had accepted Christ before being taken away. Oh, how inexpressibly sad it is to be cut off in the bloom of young womanhood like this . . .

Like this! At every pause Tuttle made, thoughts raced, the communal anger unspoken but barely contained.

—The dry goods stores were not closed, Reverend Tuttle preached with rising ire. So loud was the sobbing that his sermon was nearly inaudible at the rear of the church.

—What did he say?

—Something about the stores, I think.

—The grocery stores, the jewelry and other shops were not closed . . .

—What's he getting at?

—Hush, for God's sake—it's her funeral!

—. . . but the liquor saloons were closed in protection of a supposed criminal . . .

—*Supposed!*

—He ought to swing. He ought to.

—. . . though on other days they remain open and corrupt the innocent!

The blood was really throbbing in the breast of the blackriver town. There was no forgiveness or hope or mercy for Nell Cropsey's silent lover, Jim Wilcox. Reverend Tuttle could have kept going. Some feared he would use his moment to rekindle the lynch lust, but he pulled back and let them down gently.

He read aloud the church vows that Nell Cropsey had taken in October. Thank Thee, Lord of Hosts, that she died in Christ.

Behold, I shew you a mystery . . . at the last trump, for the trumpet shall sound; and the dead shall be raised incorruptible, and we shall be changed.

Tuttle finished, and it was done. Surely her soul was at rest. Surely her town now deserved a deep and dreamless winter sleep. They sang:

Lead, kindly Light, amid th'encircling gloom.

That night, Sunday, December 29th, 1901, the body of Nell Cropsey lay in a black walnut casket in a Sunday school room in the church annex. Across the street, a little girl was frightened and couldn't sleep. The dead body was over there in the church, and there was nothing between them except mortar and clapboards, and it was not enough.

W. O. SAUNDERS

I met every train from Elizabeth City that weekend and pestered the brakemen and conductors for news. Most of what I got turned out to be rumors.

Like the one that Jim Wilcox had been removed from Elizabeth City for safekeeping. A Pasquotank deputy claimed he took Wilcox to the Portsmouth, Virginia, jail after midnight Saturday night. And, in fact, a mud-covered carriage had discharged a handcuffed prisoner there—witnesses spread the story, and the jail was deluged with inquiries.

But Wilcox was in the Elizabeth City jail all the while, eating with relish the meals his sister Sadie brought him, saying he was comfortable and proclaiming his innocence to the man from the *Baltimore Sun*.

North Carolina officials refused to move him. He'd have to be moved up into Virginia through the Great Dismal Swamp by night, and they said they feared an escape attempt at the state line. I figured what really bothered them was the idea of turning Jim over to Virginia authorities. This case had drawn national attention, and that made Jim a hot property. Extradition could be a problem—what if the Virginia boys decided to keep Jim for themselves?

Over in Raleigh, Governor Aycock threw a fit when he heard Jim had been taken to Virginia.

—I never gave any order or permission to move Wilcox! he thundered.

But keeping him in Elizabeth City posed problems. Even after Nell's funeral, the magistrates were afraid to let Jim out on bond. The town still wasn't prepared for the sight of Wilcox walking free—he'd be lynched inside of an hour. Jim would just have to wait it out in jail, it was safer that way. In the cold before-dawn of December 30th, 1901, the bank-cashier captain of the reserves called the muster roll and dismissed the Pasquotank Rifles, who had now been standing guard two-and-a-half days.

Lawyer Aydlett waived a preliminary hearing. A third public airing of the case just then would have been futile and very unpopular. He probably thought he could get the case thrown out by the grand jury in March for lack of evidence.

—Wilcox is young and unusually cautious, he told the *Baltimore Sun*. I haven't heard any more from him than you have. He insists on his innocence and therefore doesn't fear the mob. On Friday and Saturday nights, when the jail was under guard, he was apparently the coolest man in town.

—Are you guilty? the man from the *Sun* asked Jim Wilcox.

—No, Jim said without a flinch. I am not.

JUDGE ANDREW CROPSEY

Judge Andrew Cropsey had arrived in Elizabeth City the day after Nell's body was found and had set at once about helping Solicitor Ward build his case against Wilcox. Now he was taking her back to Brooklyn to bury her among her own people.

The morning after the funeral service, the Judge had Nell's coffin packed in a white pine shipping crate and carried to the depot by the river in which they had found her.

Before they loaded her onto the train—not the regular dispatch, now, but a special train sent to carry her to Norfolk—Doctor Ike showed up with the required notice, which he dutifully tacked onto the pine box.

This is to certify that this is the body of Ella M. Cropsey who died of no disease but of violence or drowning.

Coroner Fearing

A throng met the funeral train in Norfolk late that afternoon. They watched as the pine box was lowered from the baggage car onto a waiting hearse, and they followed it to the steamer wharf. The press dogged him through the streets of Norfolk, asking what were his thoughts? And Judge Cropsey spoke freely with them all.

—Nell didn't drown herself. Why, when her body was found, the knees were drawn up just as they collapsed beneath her weight when the blow on her temple killed her. Drowned people aren't found like that and drowned women don't float face downwards. Furthermore,

—Wilcox owes his present existence to my brother. If it weren't for him, Wilcox would have surely been lynched. This Wilcox has an uncle who is said to have killed three men in cold blood. My brother is nearly distracted—all last night I could hear his sobs as he walked the floor. His wife is in a pitiable condition. No,

—I haven't seen her remains. I preferred remembering her as I last saw her—alive, well, and happy.

—What *I* think is that she was held captive till three days before her body was found, kept alive by the abductors who desired to return her. Finding themselves unable to do so, they killed her and threw her body in the river in hope her disappearance would assume the aspect of suicide.

At 6:20 the Judge and his silent charge sailed north from Norfolk on the Old Dominion steamboat.

HERBERT WYKOFF, Undertaker.

The black wagon met Judge Cropsey in the Jersey City depot the next morning, and Nell Cropsey's coffin was loaded into the Dutchman's hearse and carried across the great harbor to the New Utrecht cemetery in south Brooklyn. Judge Cropsey had brought her back from that alien swamp country, back to the place where Cropseys had been buried for a century and a half.

The Burying

Some five hundred friends, relatives, and curious strangers jammed the small graveyard. Boys climbed trees for a view. A squadron of police kept order.

The pallbearers slid the dark walnut coffin out from the heavy white curtains inside the hearse—Wykoff had torn open the pine crate at the depot and discarded it—and carried her casket to the open grave. The preacher from the church Boss Cropsey built like a fortress conducted a short service. At the head of the grave stood one of Nell's aunts, waiting to throw her large bouquet in after the coffin began its descent from the grave trestle.

But when it reached ground level, the coffin bumped, tilted sideways into the hole, and hung there at an angle.

A jolt went through the weeping crowd.

The grave was too small.

An old family grave, that of Nell Cropsey's infant brother, buried nine years before, had been opened. The gravediggers were instructed that her coffin would lie beside his; but they had left the opening too small for the casket bearing a grown woman.

Why had no one thought of this before now?

After all that had befallen her, Nell Cropsey could not even go to the earth without one last ghastly moment of delay marring that passage. Back into the hole the gravediggers went, lengthening and enlarging the grave, their shovels slicing into the hard, frozen ground of New York shook shook shook.

W. O. Saunders

All the attention over in Elizabeth City then was on the prosecutor's office. It wasn't just that everyone was depending on Solicitor Ward to see that justice was done and Jim was strung up. They were counting on Ward to tell them what had really happened.

We still didn't know. Did Jim have accomplices who kept her somewhere or had she been killed that first night and thrown straight into the river?

I read every paper I could get my hands on there in Hertford and met the westbound trains when I could steal away from the butcher shop. I couldn't hear enough about the Cropsey case.

A curious and damning story had come in from a farmer named Caleb T. Parker, who was a friend of the Wilcox family and, I understood, had gone bond for an uncle of Jim's up for murder in the 1890s.

The story went that Parker, driving his buggy home late on the night Nell Cropsey disappeared, told his wife that he had seen Jim dragging a young woman across the road in front of the Cropsey home. Parker's wife was spreading this around, and when some reporters asked Parker about it, he said that if his wife said it was so, then it was so. To other reporters, he denied the whole thing.

The thinking in the prosecutor's office was that Jim had lured Nell to the front gate, struck her, carried her to the river's edge, put her in a boat, rowed out into the Pasquotank and thrown her overboard. Jim was said to have known of three boats kept nearby at Hayman's shipyards, where he was working at that time. And there were stories circulating about a mystery skiff, supposed to have left the shore in front of the Cropsey home about quarter past eleven that night in November 1901.

But the roughest thing against Jim, as far as I could see, was his inability or unwillingness to explain how it came to be that he was seen by Leonard Owens a ten-

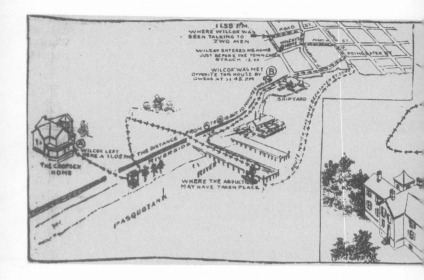

The Three Theories of Miss Nell Cropsey's Death
(from the *News and Observer*, January 7th, 1902)

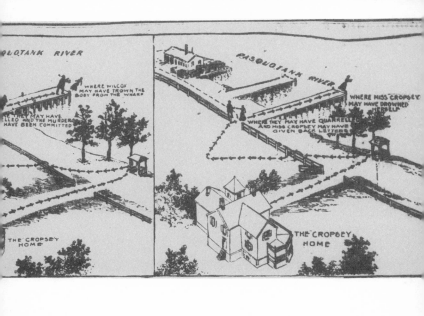

PASQUOTANK RIVER

WHERE WILCOX
MAY HAVE THROWN THE
BODY FROM THE WHARF

...HE MAY HAVE
...LLED AND THE MURDER
...HAVE BEEN COMMITTED

THE CROPSEY
HOME

PASQUOTANK RIVER

WHERE MISS CROPSEY
MAY HAVE DROWNED
HERSELF

WHERE THEY MAY HAVE QUARRELLED
AND MISS CROPSEY MAY HAVE
GIVEN BACK LETTERS

THE CROPSEY
HOME

minute walk away from the Cropsey home some *forty* minutes after he left it.

The popular notion was that there was nothing else Jim Wilcox could have been doing in that unexplained time but murdering Beautiful Nell Cropsey.

TALK

—Missus Cropsey got a anonymous letter the night before they found her girl in the river.

—What'd it say?

—*Your daughter will appear in front of your house to-morrow.*

—Well, who the hell wrote it?

—Anonymous means nobody.

—Well, I heard that whoever was guilty for it got afraid on account of the electric searchlight they ordered up for the diver to use, so the killers went on and cut her loose from the weights that were holding her down on the river bottom.

—There weren't no weights.

—Well, I got it from—

—The coroner said there weren't no weights.

—Oh.

—You see in the paper what the Committee's up to?

—What's that?

—They're saying that Chief Dawson and Mayor Wilson tried to hold em up and keep em from finding that gal when everybody was so all het up about it. They got a report she was over in Wilson and they sent off a couple of their men to go check it out—and even so, Chief Dawson wired em in Wilson to turn her loose 'cause he was sure it weren't Nell Cropsey. It weren't either.

—Harry Greenleaf say all this?

—No. He's the only one that didn't. The other four Committee men did though. You want to know what else?

—What?

—Chief Dawson and Mayor Wilson are suing the hell out of the Committee.

—For how much?

—Thousands of dollars. Thousands.

W. O. SAUNDERS

I'd badgered them for months to give me an assignment and let me write, but it came as a pretty big surprise when the story they were caught up short on was this one.

—Cover Wilcox trial for *Dispatch*.

The telegram from Norfolk came March 13th, 1902, the day they were picking a jury to try Jim Wilcox. There were no other instructions. You can bet I left Dad's meat shop and lit out for Elizabeth City in a hurry.

Two days before, an eighteen-man grand jury had spent the morning hearing from the Cropseys and the autopsy doctors in the matter of superior court docket number 19. The state was seeking a murder indictment against Jim Wilcox. His father, Tom Wilcox the former sheriff, hung around the courthouse all day talking with his old buddies and putting up a good front despite the circumstances. Lawyer Aydlett wondered even at that late date whether or not to ask for a change of venue.

Just after noon that day, Solicitor Ward was interrupted in the middle of a courtroom speech on another case. In the rear of the courtroom was a big commotion. The grand jury tramped down the center aisle toward the bench followed by a trail of spectators. The foreman lined his grand jury up and handed a paper to the judge. There was a hush in court.

—Is this paper your finding? asked the judge.

The foreman nodded it was.

After lunch the bailiff brought Jim Wilcox into court, fifteen pounds heavier than when Elizabeth City had last seen him being hauled through its streets the day Nell's body was found. He wore a short dark coat and light trousers, a clean shirt with a turned down collar and a black bow tie. At twenty-five, his hairline was receding. Just the day before, he shaved the full beard he'd grown in jail since December. Solicitor Ward ordered him to stand and remain standing as he read the grand jury finding.

—Indictment for murder, he said.

—The jurors for the State upon their oaths present, that James Wilcox with force and arm feloniously, willfully and of his malice aforethought did kill and murder Ella M. Cropsey against the statute and against the peace and dignity of the State.

The sheriff took Jim to the bar. How would he plead?

—Not guilty.

How would the defendant be tried?

—For good and evil, Lawyer Aydlett answered the court, and the trial was under way.

The judge had ordered two hundred and fifty freeholders to appear, and when I got to town Thursday afternoon, they had already started on jury selection. A ten-year-old boy had drawn the names from the county jury box—they always assumed a child would act with a hand of innocence, but I recall reading about a boy in Elizabeth City whose father sent him home to fetch a revolver when the December mobs were forming against Jim.

I was finally in on it—not just there, but there as a reporter, sitting at a press table with top-dog space writers from the big city papers. I was nearly eighteen and in on a national sensation. Elizabeth City was swarming again, the morning train down from Norfolk was packed, and farmers' wagons were parked wheel to wheel all over town.

A bevy of agents pushing farm equipment added to the crush around the courthouse square early that morning. But the main draw was a man with a Vandyke beard and mustache, pulling crowds away from the hayrake vendors as he hypnotized people, worked puppets, and threw his voice. Folks called him the Big Indian Tea Man because he rode the county-court circuit all over eastern Carolina—I knew him from Hertford—performing and peddling Indian herbal remedies and homemade philters. They said he once rode with Buffalo Bill, and now here he was in Elizabeth City.

The new courthouse itself was a great, three-story brick building with four plain white columns and Corinthian caps. The columns stood on rough-hewn granite piers, and they, in turn, supported a pediment in the center of which was a granite slab inscribed *1882*. Above that rose a cupola housing the town clock and bell.

It still stands, and we still use it.

Inside, the second-floor courtroom was an enormous box with seats like church pews, bare plaster walls, and a thin-strip slat ceiling thirty-five feet above the floor. Along the side walls were oil lamps and an occasional heat stove, and from the middle of the ceiling above the center aisle, there hung a chandelier with twelve lamps. The jury box was up front on the right.

In this room Jim's life was on the line.

For six hours that Thursday, the court went through the lists. Most of the two hundred rejected men said their minds were set against Jim Wilcox, and evidence to the contrary wouldn't make any difference to them. It was eight in the evening before they had a jury.

The twelve good men and true were a mill worker, a butcher, a veneer factory owner, a barkeep, a machinist, and seven farmers. Ten were Democrats, white men; the other two were black Republicans.

—The Wilcoxes are Republicans, people said.

—This case's too important to have nigras on the jury, they said.

—They'll come back with a hung jury or acquittal one.

You can bet the town was riled over that.

The judge ordered the jury sequestered and advised the jury officer not to let them get near any whiskey. But before they left, Solicitor Ward stood and Jim Wilcox stood and Ward said,

—These men will be called upon to pass between your life and your death. You may challenge them, any of them, and you shall be heard.

It seemed to me Jim blanched ever so slightly.

This was all more exciting than upsetting to me at the time. I didn't know Jim then.

I didn't know what lay in store.

JIM WILCOX

That W. O. Saunders kept after me ever since I come back from prison, wanting me to do a book about it with him, fifty-fifty.

If I'd just tell my side he'd write it up and print it in his newspaper shop and sell it. All I had to do was talk.

I finally said I would, thinking who knows, maybe there'd be some money in it for me.

I told him I wanted to talk where nobody'd hear us and he said we should take a boat ride upriver toward Camden. I was supposed to meet him down at the wharf one morning in the summer of 1932, but I changed my mind and didn't go.

A few days after that, my friend Cliff Madrin told me he'd spoke with W. O., who was sorry I hadn't met him but the offer still stood. It was a rainy night sometime later he got Cliff to bring him over to the shanty where me and George Madrin were living then. We heard a car door slam. I looked out and Cliff was running up through the rain. Couldn't see who the driver was.

Cliff come in dripping wet and said, It's W. O. again, Jim. I weren't much for talking that night so I lit out the back way.

He finally did catch up with me, where I don't recall, and I told him it weren't no use—everybody's expecting me to say I killed Nell Cropsey and I ain't going to say it. After that, W. O. Saunders pretty much left me alone.

W. O. SAUNDERS

I got there early the first day and sat at the press table, sharpening my dozen pencils over and over. An hour before court convened, the courtroom was filled to suffocation.

All the standing room was taken. The court floor creaked under the shifting weight of so many bodies. A dozen or so boys sat around the judge's bench at his invitation, while others, more industrious, raided the anterooms for ballot boxes, which they hawked as make-shift seats for up to a dollar apiece. The town's well-dressed women had a section to themselves within the rail. I took it all in.

Looking fresh and even relaxed, Jim came in with the jailer. The jury, having spent a sleepless night locked in the mayor's office, looked the worse for wear.

The first witness was the coroner.

Doctor Ike Fearing had been Pasquotank County coroner for three years, and even though he was young and green, the court declared him a medical expert. Solicitor Ward led him back to the day they'd found Nell Cropsey in the river, back through every gruesome detail of her public autopsy, and the people hung on every word.

Doctor Ike told how they stripped her naked and cut her wide open.

He said she was a pure virgin.

He told about blood in Nell Cropsey's swollen left temple, and how the brains ran out.

—Have you an opinion from what you saw what produced that swelling on the left temple? Solicitor Ward asked Doctor Ike.

—Objection! Lawyer Aydlett, leaping to his feet in an instant, was overruled.

—It was caused by a blow.

I ought to give Aydlett his due here. I don't know who prepped him, but he was fired up and had a strong grasp of the medical facts. The court overruled him as he doggedly objected to virtually every opinion Doctor Ike ventured. I could see he was going to have a field day with the young coroner when his turn came. It was something to watch.

—Have you an opinion, asked the solicitor, as to what kind of instrument would probably have produced a blow of that appearance?

Jim Wilcox, who they said carried a blackjack and bragged about it, chewed gum and looked bored.

—Objection! said Aydlett.

—Some round, padded instrument.

Objection, objection overruled.

—What effect would such a blow produce upon a person of her constitution and physique?

—A half hour of unconsciousness.

Objection, objection overruled. Solicitor Ward laid his medical case before the court.

—Coroner Fearing, what is indicated by the absence of water in the stomach, the lungs, and pleural cavities, and by the absence of blood in the venous, or right, side of the heart?

—Death, said Doctor Ike clearly and without hesitation, by not being drowned.

In the years since then, there's been plenty of time to reconsider the coroner's whole line. I've learned that drowning is a very complex pathological problem, and I've reached the conclusion that there is no reliable way to fix the cause of death in a body which has undergone as much postmortem change as this one. Nell Cropsey was in that river as many as thirty-seven days—too much time had passed to tell.

How was anyone to know? After all, that was the turn of the century in one small corner of the barely civilized world. When Doctor Ike and his fellows examined her and told the town she had been stricken and drowned, they believed him. When he changed his mind and laid it all on a suspected blow to the head, they changed their minds with him.

That afternoon it was Aydlett's turn, and he bore down on Doctor Ike like a northeaster on the Outer Banks.

—Look at that paper, Aydlett said, holding a copy of the coroner's report in front of the coroner himself.

—Is that your signature?

—Yes, said Doctor Ike.

—Did you find any marks of violence upon that body at that examination?

—No. Not at the first examination we made.

—Then you had a conversation with Solicitor Ward here and went back to the Cropsey barn?

—Yes.

—With the same doctors?

—Yes.

—Same jury?

—Yes.

Lawyer Aydlett stopped to let his point sink in.

—Is it not a fact, he asked, that in drowning victims there is frequently no blood in the right side of the heart?

—Sometimes.

—Then you cannot rule out drowning as a possible cause of death simply because there is no blood in the right side of the heart?

—No, said the coroner.

—Is it not a fact that forty-eight and seven-tenths percent of drowned people have no water in their lungs at all?

—I think so.

—Then you did *not* mean to tell the jury this morning that because there was no water found in Miss Cropsey's lungs, it was positive evidence that she did not drown?

—No.

Solicitor Ward must have been furious. Aydlett had backed the state's chief medical witness into a corner and was closing in.

—Now, Doctor, would not a bruise be about the same in appearance if it occurred just a few minutes before or after death, and would it not be difficult to tell whether a bruise was received ten or fifteen minutes before death or in the drowning struggles?

—That would very likely be about the same, the coroner allowed.

—Is it not a fact that the medical books you have read lay it down that bruises or marks found upon a body in the water must not create a hasty suspicion of murder?

—I think they say something like that.

—Have you ever read of an autopsy on a body which had been in the water longer than the body of Miss Cropsey?

—I don't think I have, Doctor Ike answered.

—Does not Taylor, in his medical jurisprudence, lay down this, that after the lapse of five or six weeks, even if the body is underwater, no practitioner at the present day would think of reaching final conclusions? The length of time creates doubt and uncertainty as to the cause of death, does it not?

—No. Doctor Ike was contentious. The weather has a great deal to do with it. It was very cold weather, and the body was in a perfect state of preservation.

—Do not Reese and Taylor controvert your position, Coroner?

—Yes.

—Then you tell this jury and this court that you have never seen a drowned body before, if this was not one, and yet you set your opinion against the authority you have read?

—Yes.

Aydlett fired away at Doctor Ike with a line of questioning designed to confuse the young coroner and discredit his findings. Doctor Ike was on the stand a day and a half—the court stenographer gave out after the first day, and they had to *beg* him to stay on—and Doctor Ike's concentration wilted, but he never wavered in his certainty that Nell Cropsey had been dealt a death blow that night by Jim Wilcox.

About that blow to the temple. While most of the blood in a dead body decomposes, some blood will always settle in the lowest, most dependent point of the body. If Nell Cropsey had been lying on the river bottom with her left temple at the lowest point, she would have ended up with a bruise there, exactly like the one she had. There's another little something I've become aware of in these intervening years. In the case of a male killing a female, the method of beating or striking the woman's head is rare. It is very doubtful to me that this was the method in which Nell Cropsey was murdered, *if* she were murdered. Had it been, it's doubtful still that one blow would have been enough to kill her. The most common way in which men kill women, and a very difficult method to detect, is strangulation.

It was going to be a long trial. You could see it in the faces of the jurymen, who were being kept at the Riverview Hotel with no women and no whiskey and the whole town watching.

TALK

—You hear when Chief Dawson went to Wilcox's house to get him that night there was wet clothes hanging on a peg on the back of Jim's door? He must of carried her out into the river and dumped her body to have wet clothes like that. I forget who I got that from.

—Nell Cropsey never more than just put up with Jim Wilcox. She had practically sent him packing for good. Why, she'd even asked her cousin Carrie to tell Jim she had no more use for him.

—Wilcox was in an ugly mood that night—you know he said all over town that Nell Cropsey would never go to New York?

Word spread, whipping up the townspeople and unleashing the darkness in their hearts. Along the wharves and in the warehouses and textile mills and canneries and brickyards, over what few telephone lines the town had, the word spread of Jim's certain guilt. And there was talk aplenty in the fields, for it was planting time in Pasquotank.

They were a conservative people, normally, a practical and law-abiding people who had built their town hard by a river and made it the most prosperous place in eastern Carolina, hard-working people who had turned the primeval swamps into truck farms and a riverbend into a town.

But the December fevers had returned with a fury. The rumors went to work on them in the shops and mills and saloons and kitchens and parlors and in the bedrooms. They wanted Jim Wilcox to pay for the death of Beautiful Nell Cropsey, and their talk convicted him out of court.

Women talked secretly of dressing as men and joining the lynch mob that would certainly form should Wilcox win an acquittal. One of the bolder publicly berated Lawyer Aydlett.

—If Wilcox is freed, Ed Aydlett, I hope the mob will string him up to the nearest tree—and I'll be willing to help.

Men were irate when they heard that one of the jurors

had said he was opposed to capital punishment. One man was nearly struck and beaten in a barroom because he hesitated to express his opinion about Jim Wilcox.

An impassioned youth wandered about town soaking it all up. He went to the telegraph office and wired his editor in Norfolk:

Jim Wilcox is a man without friends. It is an ominous sign.

OLLIE CROPSEY

Saint Patrick's Day was my day to go to court.

There was a cold, heavy rain falling, just as there had been during Nell's funeral. There was that banshee wind again, just as it was the night we lost her.

Mama woke me early and I dressed slowly in my black suit. I was frightened and numb over what had to be done. Papa held my dark high-collar coat for me and Mama said, Wear your black veil.

So many were there it was quite warm in the courtroom. I couldn't speak loudly enough for them to hear me, so I lifted my veil. They all leaned forward and stared.

I heard myself telling the story of a family who once lived and prospered in a beautiful part of a great city and how this family uprooted itself and came to live in a house with a tower and porches beside a wide dark river. Then I heard the dogs barking and my uncle calling my father to get his gun and I felt the bed and she wasn't there. And I cried, Don't shoot, Papa, Nell and Jim are out there yet!

I wept.

For how long I don't know, and when I recovered my

Carrie, Ollie, and Nell Cropsey

composure and looked up, the people in the courtroom were frozen and silent. Jim Wilcox never took his eyes off me. I only saw him once more in my life.

I will not mourn him.

W. O. SAUNDERS

For the longest time there was only the sound of the sobbing girl. The crowd had hung breathless on her every word and was moved. The judge himself was visibly affected. Ollie Cropsey was tall and slender, with pretty hands and, beneath her high-piled hair, a white swan neck. She was a lovely young girl—to me she was a vision. No one coughed, no one stirred, no one said a word. The emotion behind her tears was so pure than any remark would have been a blasphemy against the sovereignty she held over that moment.

Now if this trial had anything like a comic relief, it was Cale Parker, who testified that afternoon.

He'd shot off his mouth so much and changed his story so often that by the time he got on the stand, he was a public laughingstock whom no one believed. All he would allow was that he'd seen a man and a woman of about the same medium height and that there had been a second man walking some ways behind them—right in front of the Cropsey house, November 20th, 1901. It had been a bright moonlit night and the top was down on Parker's buggy, but he said he didn't recognize the man he saw with the woman. And he had known Jim a good ten years or more.

It turned out that before the trial Nell's father had taken a New York detective to see Parker. From a rough diagram they'd learned how and where Parker had seen a woman resting her head on a man's shoulder near the Cropsey home that night. But Parker's own brother claimed he could prove that Parker was over at his house before Nell ever stepped out onto the porch with Jim. I would have been inclined to dismiss Parker altogether, except for Carrie Cropsey's testimony. She had gone up to bed between ten-thirty and quarter to eleven and had seen a buggy pass by some ten or fifteen minutes later. Now that could have been Parker's buggy. And if more time had elapsed than Carrie remembered, Parker was there at just the right time. As to what he saw, if anything, you could take your pick.

Beyond that, there was only speculation.

Before the trial, Solicitor Ward floated the story that a Negro named Thompson was prepared to swear he saw Jim Wilcox cross the road just in front of him carrying a limp young woman toward the river. Thompson had been holding back because he was afraid Jim would kill him. He could have been the other man Parker saw.

Thompson never testified.

And there was the rumor that a Negro—Thompson?—would take the stand to disclose a conspiracy between certain well-known persons not theretofore mentioned in connection with the case. That witness never materialized, either.

I caught up with Parker in the street outside the courthouse after he testified. He was in a big hurry.

—It's reported, I said, that you told your wife you saw Jim Wilcox dragging the body of a woman toward the water.

—I told her some time after, when this thing came out, that I saw somebody *might* be him but I thought nothing of it. That nigger that works for me—he tried to get me into a terrible mess. I got to be going.

And Cale Parker took off down Main Street.

I went back to the press table and watched Jim Wilcox even more closely. Everything was against him and yet he sat through the whole business as if he were the most disinterested spectator. I had read up on Lombroso's theory of the born criminal and decided maybe that's what Wilcox was—a throwback, a reversion, a congenital killer.

The eighteen-year-old with a sensational murder case for his first job had a big imagination. There was plenty to feed it.

I asked around and didn't hear one favorable word about Jim. The Norfolk papers reported heavy wagering there on the trial's outcome: bets of hundreds of dollars, with odds two to one that if Jim got the first degree he'd break down on the gallows and name his accomplice. The feeling in Elizabeth City was that the evidence was inconclusive, but still public sentiment grew stronger and more bitter against Jim Wilcox as the trial ground on hour after hour.

A strong current of denunciation of Jim ran through William Cropsey's testimony on Tuesday, March 18th. When he stepped down from the stand, the audience broke into cheers and thunderous, protracted applause. Judge Jones gaveled hard and threatened to clear the court.

Then it was the defense's turn to call witnesses, and the crowd was going to get what it came for—Jim Wilcox's firsthand account of what he did between eleven and midnight that night. Probably no more than a handful outside of Jim's family was prepared to believe a word he'd say even under oath, but everyone wanted to see how this cold creature would behave on the stand.

Jim stunned us all.

I bolted down the center aisle ahead of the rest, raced

to the wire office on Poindexter Street, shoved a dictionary in front of the telegrapher and told him to send *it* till I got my story written. The other reporters were plenty heated at the way I'd tied up the only telegraph line out of town. I wired the *Dispatch* in Norfolk a story the gist of which was this:

E. F. Aydlett, defense counsel in the most widely publicized criminal case in North Carolina history, will neither call witnesses nor present evidence.

Jim Wilcox, on trial for his life in a case still shrouded in mystery, will not take the stand in his own defense.

JIM WILCOX

Early on the morning of December 4, 1934, the sick old sandy-haired man Jim Wilcox scrounged three #6 shotgun shells, jimmied the lock to Johnny Tuttle's office, and stole a twelve-gauge shotgun. He lay on his dirty bunk listening to the freight trains rumble and couple not far away.

Johnny Tuttle and his family, all of em, have been good to me. To think his wife was one of the last people I saw, that little girl in 1903, before I went off to prison, and there she was at the station with Johnny and her children the day I come back in 1918. That's been sixteen years now.

It was rough when I first got out. I shouldn't of come back here but there was nowhere else to go. I'd been a volunteer fireman before so I went over to the firehouse and Chief Flora gave me a paying job—one of two live-in firemen Elizabeth City had. I kept a monkey and let him ride on my shoulder. Well, a fire alarm come in one day and I missed it. Chief Flora said I'd been slack and he couldn't take chances like that. He fired me, but I didn't care. I was always getting in fights around there anyway. People wouldn't leave me alone.

Seems I been drifting ever since. My grocery went under, and it's just been odd jobs and drinking. Folks say I'm real good with my hands. Real good with my hands and my tools. Some tell me I'm light on my feet.

I come back into town from Kelly Tillet's fish camp last April, and Johnny Tuttle partitioned me off a little room in back of his car repair shop. Ain't it something, my sister lives right over on the next street and don't even come see me with a hot meal now I'm old and sick? She met me crying at the depot how glad she was to see me home all those years ago, and took what money I'd made selling carved canes and wallets and such—a couple thousand dollars—and told me she'd apply it to the house and I could live there the rest of my life.

It weren't a year later she threw me out.

I been getting pretty bad with the cough this fall. Johnny Tuttle went and gave my sister a piece of his mind but it didn't do any good. He's a good heart. It hurt me when he got sharp with me last summer for blaspheming.

I was standing in front of the garage when a storm come up and there was a great thunderclap. I pulled a quarter out of my pocket and flipped it and said,

—Give me another quarter's worth.

I'd barely got the words out when there was a second thunderclap even louder than the first. Johnny Tuttle he rolled out from under the car he was working on and said real fierce,

—Don't you let me hear you talk like that again around here. I mean it.

I don't want the Tuttles getting mad at me, so mostly I been staying in my back room. A Sawyer fellow asked me to go to church in November but I said no thanks. I'd been up to the First Baptist Church and two people got up and moved across the aisle. I don't want any of it.

People don't want me around. Everybody whispers and looks down on me. I told Tuttle's wife time and again there weren't much point in going on living. There was a crowd around the garage a few weeks ago. I was drinking and got hold of Tuttle's shotgun. I told em, Look out I'm going tp end it all, and the gun went off into the rafters. They all laughed at me except Tuttle, who was mad again.

—Don't mess with my gun anymore. From now on, I'm locking up my shells in the house when I come in from hunting.

Nobody'll ever know where I got these three shells.

I gave em warning day before yesterday. I let one of Tuttle's mechanics have a pair of my overalls and gave one of the other boys a spare shirt and told em I won't be needing em much longer.

People don't want me around all right. I know who killed Nell Cropsey, and I always said I was going to tell everything I know before I die.

THE LAWYERS

For two-and-a-half days, the lawyers made dramatic, tearful, imploring speeches. Those were the days, it would later be said, of the great trial lawyers.

Solicitor Ward compared the case to that of Cluverius, a young Virginia lawyer convicted of murder and hanged in front of cheering mobs in Richmond fifteen years earlier. Cluverius accounted for all but six minutes of his time on the night a girl he barely knew met her death in the Belle Isle reservoir, and still they executed him. Jim Wilcox had the better part of an hour to explain.

—The eyes of the world are on this jury, Ward proclaimed. Would it not be an eternal disgrace for North Carolina if this inhuman wretch went free to murder more of our precious girls?

In whispers, the prosecution painted the murder scene and the recovery of Nell's body till there was not a dry eye in the Pasquotank County Courthouse. Hundreds strained to see some sign of guilt from Jim Wilcox.

—If the trees could talk, if the wind and stars could talk, they could tell who put her in that river, Ward concluded. But Jim Wilcox is the only one who can.

Wilcox sat unmoved and expressionless. The town was amazed.

When Lawyer Aydlett began his defense, three hundred people stood en masse and marched out of the courtroom by design. The word had been passed—there would be a walkout to break the force of his argument. Aydlett started anew, but within fifteen minutes the fire bell rang out, and those still in the courtroom ran to the tall side windows. The boiler wagon, followed by the hose carts, clattered down Main Street. But there was no fire.

Jim Wilcox sucked on a lemon—as if he had heard that was what Stonewall did in battle—and ignored the commotion.

Lawyer Aydlett said Jim had barely ten minutes to account for—hadn't Roy Crawford told Ollie Cropsey at 11:30 that Nell and Jim were in the hall yet? Then, ten minutes or so later, Jim met Len Owens at a point that was a ten-minute walk from the Cropsey house, spoke briefly and nonchalantly, and walked on to the corner of Shepard and Road, where he was seen talking with two men just before midnight. It all timed out perfectly in establishing Jim's innocence. There had been no motive —there had been no time.

—The pictures Jim returned which were undiscovered are probably at the bottom of the Pasquotank, Aydlett suggested. Miss Cropsey, distraught over the attentions Jim had been paying her cousin Carrie, walked across the rivershore road, down the pier that Hurricane Branch's bloodhounds had tracked, and threw herself into the river and drowned. The sad, simple truth of the case was that Nell Cropsey's death was suicide.

—Why would Wilcox have left all the doors to the Cropsey house open when Nell came out on the porch? Surely he would have closed them as a minimal precaution had he planned to murder Nell Cropsey. And why would he have waited so late in the evening, when he must have known Roy Crawford would be leaving shortly? Murder is not only highly implausible; murder has not been proven. The circumstantial evidence is not strong enough—you must acquit Jim Wilcox.

The town clock in the courthouse cupola struck five as Aydlett finished.

Jim Wilcox pulled out his gold watch and checked the time.

W. O. SAUNDERS

The judge was hoarse from the strenuous trial, and he rasped his instructions to the jury a week after Doctor Ike had given the opening testimony. Try the case as

men, the judge said. Get up above public opinion, lest
you do violence to your oaths.

Friday, March 21st, 1902, was a warm spring day in
Betsy Town, and men and women stood about the street
corners and hotel lobbies awaiting the verdict.

I heard toasts drunk to Jim's execution.

The jury's deliberation dragged like a wounded snake
on into Friday night. A gang of laborers and stevedores
got nearly worked up enough to attack the jury quarters
in the Riverview Hotel and demand a verdict at once.

In a barbershop on Saturday morning, word was that
the jury stood locked eight to four for hanging. Someone
else said no, it was ten to two.

I heard a well-dressed out-of-towner say he hadn't
come to Elizabeth City for any damned foolishness. He
had come to see Jim Wilcox lynched.

I saw Tom Wilcox running back and forth across
town, taking this one and that one aside for a quick
word,

—Who are they? Tell me, goddamn it, or I'll break
you in half.

He was desperate to find out who the lynch leaders
were, and there was no concealing it. I learned that
Chief Dawson had a carriage waiting ready to spirit Jim
out of town at a moment's notice. Every nerve in town
was on the stretch.

I'd never seen people act like this before. I had never
felt that tight-gut feeling either, but it was powerful and
contagious. There was no escaping or shaking it. I was a
reporter doing a pretty good job for the first time out, but
another feeling got to me that Saturday while the Wilcox
jury was out.

I was afraid, and I wanted to go home.

OLLIE CROPSEY

I think we learn almost from birth the sadness of the tolling bell. Where we live now at the edge of town, the sound of the bells is very faint.

The town clock rang ten o'clock but didn't stop, a signal, Papa said, that the jury was coming in at last after thirty-six hours. He left for the courthouse, alone in the moonlight.

Waiting up for Papa, I lay back on the lounge and closed my eyes. I tried not to weep over it any more, but I failed. I tried to be calm and tell myself it didn't matter what the jury ruled. In my mind I passed judgment upon Jim and upon myself. I loved Nell deeply, and he took her from me and our family. I loved her, and I let her go.

You know what you have done, Jim Wilcox. And no matter what, you will suffer and you will pay even as I have.

Even as I.

JIM WILCOX

Oil-light shadows danced on the courtroom walls, grotesque distended images, and amid the flickering, a weird yellow glow fell on every face. Spectators trembled from suspense, while outside men waited with a coiled rope.

—Have you reached a verdict?

—We have.

—The prisoner will rise and face the jury.

So ordered, he stood like a statue, pale even in that light, and with a military precision turned and looked the jury full in the eye.

—What is your verdict?

—Guilty.

Jim's father looked from the jury to the judge and back again, as if he had misunderstood.

—In what degree?

He must pay, thought Nell's father, to the full measure of the law.

—In the first degree.

Solicitor Ward buried his head in his hands. Lawyer Aydlett wept openly. Still Jim didn't flinch, but rather walked without a tremor and stood before the judge.

—It is sadder for me than you, but I must sentence you on April twenty-fifth next to be taken from the county jail and carried to a public place between the hours of ten and three and hanged by the neck till dead.

He showed no reaction, nor any trace of emotion, and as the sheriff led him away to jail, the prosecutor said almost in disbelief,

—He has the most remarkable nerve I ever saw.

Well I'm sick now, maybe with the TB again, and I'm sick of this town and how they whisper and point.

I been holed up in this room long enough.

It was no trouble to break in early this morning and get that shotgun. They say you don't even hear the noise, so let somebody else feel guilty for a change—it's no trouble to get real comfortable and wonder what they'll make of it and put the muzzle tight up against my chin and just go on and pull the trigger.

Gene Betts was pulling a tire off a car when he heard the report of the shotgun. Old Jim's shooting up the roof again, he thought. When he walked around back ten minutes later, he was staggered by what he saw through the back room window.

Jim's head was shot away.

In the grimy back room were just a table and a bunk built into the wall. Two or three hard biscuits lay on the table. Over the mattress was a raggedy, soiled quilt, and at the foot of the bed an old overcoat Tuttle had given Jim. The pillow was soaked with brains and blood. Later someone found a small piece of skull and tied it to a string and hung it from a rafter in Tuttle's garage, a grim memento of Jim Wilcox.

W. O. SAUNDERS

Jim's suicide evoked a certain amount of sympathy in Elizabeth City, and it stirred up the town's old memories and old talk about the Nell Cropsey case. Some folks believed that surely this was proof of Jim's guilt, an admission that he could no longer live with himself and the awful burden of his crime. Others took it to be the last statement from an innocent man scorned and disbelieved and hounded to the grave.

Then the dark stories came pouring forth, rumors and theories some of which had lain unspoken for years.

Among the most persistent was the notion that William Cropsey had killed his own daughter. It was a hair-raising thought, but even people who believed in Jim's guilt were willing to entertain it out of some irresistible fascination.

In one version, Cropsey found Nell embracing his neighbor John Fearing—the very man whose advertisement had brought the Cropseys to the South—and as he attacked Fearing with a singletree, Nell stepped between the two men and caught the blow. Fearing and Cropsey then found themselves in an unholy alliance to conceal a double conspiracy—adultery and murder—

and Jim, who had gone home hours earlier, was left to take the blame.

Yet William Cropsey is said to have stopped in at the Fearing home on his way back from the Wilcox house that night, and John Fearing, awakened and alarmed, joined Cropsey in his search.

Others heard that Cropsey came out onto the porch that night while Nell and Jim were still together and slapped her around in a violent argument. Jim left before it was resolved. Josh Dawson saw a light burning in the attic tower of Seven Pines during the long period of Nell's disappearance, and he and others speculated that Nell was being kept, dying, up there in the attic. Clothier D. Walter Harris believed Cropsey had hidden her body in his icehouse for some time before putting her in the river.

Implausible as they were, these stories would not die.

Some heard a tale concocted by a pulp detective magazine that had Jim conspiring with Ollie's suitor Roy Crawford and with Ollie and Nell's younger brother Will. They kidnapped Nell, possibly with her approval, hoping to collect ransom enough to cover their gambling debts at a Norfolk horse track, but something went wrong—Nell was killed and abandoned to the Pasquotank. After all, hadn't Roy Crawford gone near mad and shot himself in 1908? And hadn't Will Cropsey poisoned himself in 1913?

And now Jim.

No one remembers much about Roy Crawford, but Will Cropsey's bleak end attracted a great deal of attention. It seems he came home drunk and depressed one night in Norfolk. He had lost a job with one railroad several months earlier, and though he'd just hired on with another line, he was miserable with his wife and five-year-old daughter and was drinking heavily. He offered to shoot the two of them and himself, but instead, right in front of them, he sat and drained a bottle of carbolic acid and was dead in minutes.

I doubt it had anything to do with Jim and Nell. The Cropseys were a family whom tragedy had inexplicably visited twice inside of fifteen years. At the time of Jim's death, they became a subject of public curiosity once again.

For years Jim had whispered to various ones in his family and around his Church Street haunts that he would tell all he knew before he died. And since he had never said one word at either of his trials—for Lawyer Aydlett did get him a second trial in 1903—the myth grew up that Jim knew more, much more than ever came out in court. He realized this, and he played on that myth. When word flew through town that Jim had killed himself, what *everyone* wanted to know was,

—Did he leave a note?
—Did he name the killer?
—Did he *confess*?

Kelly Tillet came into my office just after Jim's death and told me Jim had done a lot of writing when he stayed at the Tillet place in south Pasquotank, and Jim had buried these writings in a tin box near the house. I made the mistake of printing Kelly's hoax in *The Independent*, and when he took his wife back to the country they found their house ransacked, mattresses slit, downfeathers everywhere—even flowers dumped out of their pots by someone searching for whatever Jim might have written.

Some Kitty Hawk fishermen say Jim had drifted down to the Outer Banks to fish in 1933. One of these told of rowing out into the sound with him one summer night, where Jim staked and sank an oil bag with a box of writings inside. That fall, a great hurricane carried the stake away and the writings were lost.

I don't believe it. If Jim had really wanted to do any writing, I think he would have gone on and let me put out that book with him in 1932. As long as he didn't, though, he could always corral someone into listening to his sad story, because of course no one ever knew what he might come out with or when.

It was odd and ironic that a new coroner had been sworn in the day before Jim killed himself, no stranger to the dead man whose suicide was his first case. In 1901, as a member of Doctor Ike's coroner's jury, he had noticed a crucial swelling on Nell Cropsey's left temple. In 1934, Coroner J. B. Ferebee, the barber, found only a cigarette butt, a fine-tooth comb, and two razor blades on Jim's body—no letter, note, or diary either confessing or denying the crime that had wrecked his life.

Jim Wilcox, the silent lover, the despondent drunk, was dead. He had never joined the search for his lost Nell, and many thought he never mourned her, so cold and indifferent was his heart. And yet he kept a photograph of her on his prison wall, a lock of her hair in his Bible.

He had survived lynch mobs twice. His lawyer appealed his death sentence, and the state supreme court threw out the whole first trial because of the walkout and the false fire alarm. For months Jim was held in Pasquotank County jail awaiting a new trial. When some friends dynamited a hole in the jail wall through which he could have escaped, he surprised them and stayed put. He was going to get off in court, he said.

People fled Perquimans County in droves to avoid jury duty in that second, relocated trial in January 1903.

But the trial itself was well attended, almost a replay of the first. This time, though, Aydlett was a spellbinder. When he finished his jury speech, he was roundly applauded. The jury deliberated twenty hours. When the verdict came in, both Jim's and Nell's parents were waiting at the Hertford depot to catch the train back to Elizabeth City. They got word over the station telephone that Jim had been convicted of second-degree murder and sentenced to thirty years in prison. Governor Bickett pardoned him in 1918, but Jim pulled his own time right up till the morning he blew his head off with that shotgun.

His two sisters and a small crowd were there when Jim was buried in Hollywood Cemetery, Elizabeth City, on December 5th, 1934. The preacher read a little from John 14:

> Even the Spirit of truth; whom the world cannot receive, because it seeth him not, neither knoweth him; but ye know him; for he dwelleth with you, and shall be in you.
>
> I will not leave you comfortless: I will come to you. . . . Arise, let us go hence.

It was a funeral without music.

All my life I have pondered over this story—there is only one thing more to add. Two weeks before he shot himself, Jim Wilcox telephoned me. He said,

—Mister Saunders, I'm ready to talk if you want to come over.

I had waited for that moment since the first trial. It was a cold night, so I bundled up and went on over to Tuttle's garage, where for several hours he talked about that moonlit night in November 1901. My family was waiting up for me when I got home, and I was able to tell my wife and children that I finally knew what really happened. But the price of Jim's telling me was my solemn promise to keep to myself what he revealed in confidence, thirty-three years to the night after Nell Cropsey vanished.

I never told a soul.

Men in a truck following watched the Norfolk-bound automobile swerve left off the Canalbank Highway and run a hundred feet along the shoulder before plunging into the Dismal Swamp Canal. It took several hours to dredge the car out of the eighteen-foot-deep canal that afternoon in late April 1940. The driver must have had a stroke or a heart attack, lost control of the vehicle, and then drowned, it was ruled. W. O. Saunders carried the secret of the mystery of Beautiful Nell Cropsey with him to his death beneath the dark madeira waters of the old boatway.

CHRONOLOGY

1876   Jim Wilcox born in Pasquotank County, eastern
North Carolina.

1880   Olive (Ollie) Cropsey, third child and daughter, born
into prominent Brooklyn family, descendants of early
Dutch settlers of New York.

1881   Ella Maud (Nell) Cropsey born in Brooklyn.

Elizabeth City and Norfolk Railroad opens.

1884   W. O. Saunders born in Perquimans County, adjacent
to Pasquotank on the west.

1894   James Wilcox, Jim's uncle, kills pollkeeper at
Newbegun in south Pasquotank and pleads
self-defense. Convicted of murder the next year
after sensational trial, he is acquitted by the state
supreme court the year following that.

1898   William Cropsey moves his family to Pasquotank
County from Brooklyn. Jim Wilcox, son of
the Republican county sheriff, takes up with
Nell Cropsey.

1899   Rebuilt Dismal Swamp Canal opens after three-and-
a-half years.

1901   Nell Cropsey vanishes on November 20; she is found
thirty-seven days later, dead, in the Pasquotank
River. Jim Wilcox is jailed and guarded by reserves
called out by the governor. Nell's father disperses
the lynch mob.

Elizabeth City's population triples since the coming
of the railroad.

1902   Jim Wilcox is convicted in Elizabeth City of first-degree murder and sentenced to hang for Nell's death. A mistrial is declared by the state supreme court because of public disturbances during the trial.

1903   Wilcox is retried in Perquimans County, convicted of second-degree murder, and sentenced to thirty years in prison. The Cropseys leave Seven Pines. Ollie begins reclusion.

1908   Roy Crawford, Ollie's caller on the night Nell disappeared, shoots himself to death.

        W. O. Saunders launches newspaper, *The Independent*, in Elizabeth City.

1913   Will Cropsey Jr., one of Nell's younger brothers, poisons himself to death in Norfolk, Virginia.

1918   Governor Bickett visits Jim Wilcox at mountain prison farm, pardons him several weeks later. Jim returns to Elizabeth City on Christmas Eve.

1932   Jim and W. O. Saunders plan to collaborate on a book about the Cropsey case, but Jim backs out.

1934   Jim summons W. O. to his room to talk. Two weeks later, Wilcox commits suicide.

1937   W. O. shuts down *The Independent*.

1938   William H. Cropsey dies.

1940   W. O. Saunders dies when his car swerves into the Dismal Swamp Canal.

1944   Ollie Cropsey dies.

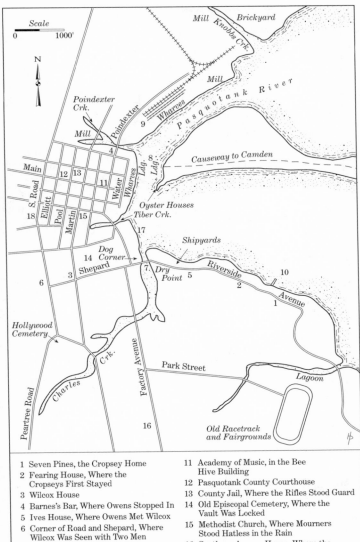

Scale
0   1000'

N

Poindexter Crk.

Mill Knobbs Crk.

Brickyard

Mill

Pasquotank River

Poindexter

Wharves

9

Mill

4

Causeway to Camden

Main

12   13

11

Water   Wharves

Ldg.   Ldg.

8

S. Road

Elliott

Pool

Martin

18

15

Oyster Houses
Tiber Crk.

17

Shipyards

Dog Corner

14

Shepard

3

7

Dry Point

5

Riverside

2

10

1

Avenue

6

Hollywood Cemetery

Charles Crk.

Factory Avenue

Park Street

Lagoon

Peartree Road

16

Old Racetrack and Fairgrounds

1   Seven Pines, the Cropsey Home
2   Fearing House, Where the Cropseys First Stayed
3   Wilcox House
4   Barnes's Bar, Where Owens Stopped In
5   Ives House, Where Owens Met Wilcox
6   Corner of Road and Shepard, Where Wilcox Was Seen with Two Men
7   Charles Creek Swivel Bridge
8   Ferry over the Narrows
9   Pennsylvania Depot
10   Pier, Where the Bloodhounds Led Hurricane Branch

11   Academy of Music, in the Bee Hive Building
12   Pasquotank County Courthouse
13   County Jail, Where the Rifles Stood Guard
14   Old Episcopal Cemetery, Where the Vault Was Locked
15   Methodist Church, Where Mourners Stood Hatless in the Rain
16   Southern Avenue House, Where the Cropseys Lived Later On
17   R. C. Abbot Co. Wharf, Where W. O. Waited for Jim
18   Tuttle's Garage

Map 1. *Elizabeth City, North Carolina*

Map 2. *Eastern North Carolina and Tidewater Virginia*

ACKNOWLEDGMENTS

One afternoon in the late 1950s, my mother, Dorothy Page Simpson, took me over to the Pasquotank River to see the deserted, vine-covered Cropsey house, my teacher Audrey Austin having just read our fourth-grade class in Elizabeth City the Nell Cropsey chapter from John Harden's *The Devil's Tramping Ground and Other North Carolina Mystery Stories*. And my late father, attorney Martin Bland Simpson, Jr., took me along with him many times into the same Pasquotank County Courthouse where Jim Wilcox once stood trial.

Two decades later in Elizabeth City, my great-aunt Jennie Simpson Overman and local historian Fred L. Fearing both graciously toured the community with me in search of the Cropsey story. Among those I spoke with about the case there (and elsewhere) were: N. Elton Aydlett; Caroline Cropsey Bartron (Cedar Creek, N.C.); E. O. (Jack) Baum; Garland Dunstan; Ethelyn Tillet Eves; Wilson Eves; Rob and Lel Fearing; Nancy Meekins Ferebee; Sudie Tillet Fulcher; John Harden (Greensboro, N.C.); D. Walter Harris; the Arthur Hemphills; Margaret Fearing Jackson; B. Culpepper Jennette, Jr.; Jack Jennette; Chief of Police W. C. Owens; Daniel W. Patterson (Chapel Hill, N.C.); Gladys Cropsey Perkins; Billie Saunders Smith; Keith Saunders (Washington, D.C.); Edna Morrisette Wood Shannonhouse; the Dwight Sylvesters; Evelyn Dawson Tuttle (Havelock, N.C.); Sam Twiford; and Boots Ziegler.

Several special collections yielded invaluable materials— court records, local newspapers, commercial appeals—that helped me both to reconstruct the story and to establish a sense of coastal Carolina life around 1900: the North Carolina Collection at the University of North Carolina in Chapel Hill, under both William S. Powell and H. G. Jones; the Sargent Room at the Norfolk Public Library, Norfolk, Va.; the North Carolina State Archives, Raleigh, N.C.; and the private library of coastal historian David Stick, then at Southern Shores, N.C., now housed at the Outer Banks History Center, Manteo, N.C. These books also proved useful: *Pasquotank Historical Society Yearbook*, volumes 1-3; *On the Shores of the Pasquotank*, by Thomas R. Butchko; *A Pictorial History of Elizabeth City, N.C.*, by Fred L. Fearing, Edward Fearing, and Gloria J. Berry; and *The Independent Man*, by Keith Saunders.

In Washington, D.C., Frank Queen went through turn-of-the-century big-city newspapers with me in the Library of Congress Periodicals Collection. And in Brooklyn, N.Y., Homer Foil joined me in looking for Cropseys in the Long Island Historical Society's library and in the old graveyard of the New Utrecht Reform Church. Others helpful in the North were Charles Lood and the Reverend Pangburn of New Utrecht Reform Church, Catherine Van Brunt, James Cropsey, William Keppel, and Henry C. Smith.

Dr. Page Hudson, Jr., former chief medical examiner of North Carolina, reviewed the medical evidence in the 1902 trial transcript, and journalist-novelist Loyd Little also worked through the intricacies of the case with me.

Novelists Doris Betts and Lee Smith allowed me to present material from early versions of this work to their creative writing classes at the University of North Carolina at Chapel Hill. Literary agent Roberta Pryor was taken with the story from the first, and my editor David Perry has shown once again how deeply he shares my and my family's love for eastern North Carolina and all its wonder and mystery.

Jerry Leath Mills has read and commented upon every draft of this work; for his encouragement, wisdom, and friendship over twenty-five years, I am forever in his debt.

To these people I offer my deepest gratitude, to all the living and the dead.

ILLUSTRATION CREDITS

Beautiful Nell Cropsey,
from the *New York Journal and American*

Jim Wilcox, from the Philadelphia *Inquirer*

Seven Pines, from the *Charlotte Observer*

W. O. Saunders, from the North Carolina Collection,
University of North Carolina at Chapel Hill

The Narrows, from *Kramers: 90 Years in the
Lumber Business in Elizabeth City, North Carolina*;
unpublished, illustrated typescript compiled by
Frank K. Kramer, 1967; copy in the North Carolina
Collection, University of North Carolina at
Chapel Hill

The Three Theories, from the *News and Observer*,
Raleigh, North Carolina, January 7th, 1902

Carrie, Ollie, and Nell Cropsey, from the *New York
Journal and American*